KILL ME, DARLING

A MIKE HAMMER NOVEL

MORE MIKE HAMMER
FROM TITAN BOOKS

KILL ME, DARLING

A MIKE HAMMER NOVEL

MICKEY SPILLANE
and
MAX ALLAN COLLINS

TITANBOOKS

Kill Me, Darling: A Mike Hammer Novel
Print edition ISBN: 9781783291397
E-book edition ISBN: 9781783291410

Published by Titan Books
A division of Titan Publishing Group Ltd
144 Southwark St, London SE1 0UP

First mass market edition: February 2016

1 3 5 7 9 10 8 6 4 2

A CIP catalogue record for this title is available from the British Library.

Printed and bound in the United States.

In memory of
HAROLD COOKE
who rode the moonshine roads
with Mickey

CO-AUTHOR'S NOTE

Shortly before his death, Mike Hammer's creator Mickey Spillane paid me an incredible honor. He asked me to complete the Hammer novel that was currently in progress—*The Goliath Bone*—and then instructed his wife Jane to gather all of the other unfinished, unpublished material and give it to me: "Max will know what to do." He described what would follow as a "treasure hunt," as these manuscripts spanned his entire career from the late '40s until his passing in 2006.

The manuscripts were substantial—usually 100 pages or more, with plot and character notes and sometimes roughed-out final chapters. Most of the books had been announced by Mickey's publisher at various times from the 1950s through the '90s. As a Spillane/Hammer fan since my early teens, I am delighted to finally see these long-promised books lined up on a shelf next to the thirteen Hammer novels published by Mickey in his lifetime.

In addition to the substantial novel manuscripts mentioned above, a number of shorter Mike Hammer manuscripts were uncovered in the treasure hunt conducted by Jane Spillane, my wife Barb and me, ranging over three offices in Mickey's South Carolina home. Some of these were fragments of a few pages, primarily the openings of never-written novels or stories; these I have been gradually turning into short stories with an eventual collection in mind. Others were more substantial if less so than the six novel manuscripts. Although they vary in particulars, these shorter but still significant unfinished manuscripts are essentially the opening chapters of novels, sometimes with character and plot notes (and, in one case, a draft of the ending).

I am setting out to complete at least three of these significant Hammer novels-in-progress, and *Kill Me, Darling* is the first. The novel is of particular interest because it is an early, variant version of Hammer's 1962 "comeback" novel, *The Girl Hunters*, in which Mike discovers that Velda—missing and thought dead for seven years—has been behind the Iron Curtain on dangerous CIA business. (The posthumous *Complex 90* is a sequel to that novel.)

Mickey's manuscript of *Kill Me, Darling* begins with the opening pages of *The Girl Hunters*, in which a drunken Hammer is dragged by cops ("They found me in the gutter") to the home of Captain Pat Chambers.

At that point, the manuscript goes in an entirely different direction, as you will see. Internal evidence indicates *Kill Me, Darling* was begun as a follow-up to *Kiss Me, Deadly*, likely around 1953 or '54, the time frame I've used for the narrative.

Rather than reuse the first few pages of *The Girl Hunters*, I have based the opening of *Kill Me, Darling* on another Spillane fragment from the same era that covered similar territory.

Many readers have asked me if I will ever write my own Mike Hammer novel. The answer is that there is no need: Mickey left behind so much wonderful unpublished material that I am privileged to continue our collaboration.

M.A.C.

CHAPTER ONE

It was quiet and dark and half-past three in the morning. The winos and the dipsos were happy things all nestled together in their doorways, and on the streets an occasional taxi would cruise by, slowing down for subway exits and still-open gin mills.

What noise was left over from the night before had been dampened by the belly rumblings of thunder over the river and a wet heat had crowded in above the city like a hand dipped in slime.

Sometimes a sudden momentary brilliance would light the sky, and down on earth below all the trouble would stand out in quick stark relief, long enough to be seen, not long enough to be perceived, much less remembered.

And when I reached the end of the block, near the river, all the trouble left in the world seemed to belong to me alone. I was walking slow but not steady—too much booze for that. But at least I looked like myself again, trenchcoat collars up and hat brim down. Both garments clean over a rumpled, soiled, torn suit that was the uniform of the barfly I'd become.

I hadn't even heard about the mugging turned murder till a week after it happened. I hadn't been much for following the papers since Velda walked out, and the kind of slop chutes I frequented couldn't afford TVs up over the counter. So it took another drunk to say, "Didn't you used to know that cop?"

"What cop? I know lots of damn cops."

"Manley? Wade Manley?"

"What about him?"

"Somebody killed him last week."

The sand was still there on the sidewalk, spread out in a wide circle. Sand scuffed and dirty now, paraded through by kids and bypassed by their elders. Sand that still had its abrasive quality but also the discoloration of old rust.

Only it wasn't rust. It was blood. Or anyway it had been. Now it was just a substance decomposed to its chemical make-up. Not so long ago it had been bright red and completely alive and the one who had carried it in his veins and had it pumping through his heart had been as big and as prominent as the stain he had left by way of remembrance.

They called Wade Manley the Big Man, and it was no exaggeration. Six three, broad-shouldered, he'd come up via the streets as a kid and later as a beat cop and when Pat Chambers and I were at the academy together, the Big Man had sought us out. You saw a heavy-set, bucket-headed guy and thought what a fat slob, but you were wrong, because despite the belly there was power in those arms and that bull neck. Those tree-trunk legs could run after you much faster than you'd ever imagine and then kick the ever-loving crap out of you, with the kind of force that only a big man could muster.

He'd come around to give a lecture on the perils and rewards of working vice, and his eyes had fixed on Pat and me in the audience.

"After you fellas put in a few years on the street," he'd said later, in a gruff friendly way, "come see me. You got the kind of faces I can use."

We asked him what he meant.

"Well, you, kid," he'd said to Chambers, "have the kind of fresh-faced look that works out great on undercover assignments. You look like somebody who just fell off the turnip truck, and that's perfect for working vice."

This had made me laugh, but the laugh caught when the Big Man looked at me and said, "And you, Hammer—you're just the kind of mean-looking roughneck who can go undercover with any evil bunch of sons of bitches, and fit right in."

And that had made Pat laugh.

This afternoon, at my office, where I hadn't been in a while, the papers had piled up. I'd quickly picked out the one with Wade Manley's picture on the front page, and a story that focused on the tough waterfront area where even a big, experienced off-duty police officer could fall prey to "malefactors." Fancy word for the kind of rats that emerged from alleyways with greedy glowing eyes and bared feral teeth, only with switchblades to do the tearing.

Eight deep punctures to his body, any one of which would have been fatal. Overkill, some might call it. Others might say thorough.

When the front-page photo was taken, the Big Man hadn't had any departmental recognition yet and the hat riding his skull looked fresh and new, almost G.I. in its crispness. He looked young and much lighter but then the picture was a dozen years old. He looked decent because he was and always had been, despite the soul-eating nature of working Vice.

And most of all he looked like a hard man to break because he was that too… and died proving it.

This I knew because the Big Man was not the sort who would just hand over his wallet to punks with knives or zip guns. They would have to take it from him. And they apparently had. And he was dead now. Stupid? Proud? Maybe. But I'd have done the same damn thing.

Only… what had he been doing down here, alone? Was this really just a mugging gone horribly wrong? Manley hadn't been on the streets himself in many years. He was strictly supervisory. Was he meeting someone?

Then, like the man said, the rains came. Came down

straight and hard as if from a giant showerhead and then I was looking at the big wide irregular discolored splotch of sand on the sidewalk as the rust color got red again and for a second the whole splotch seemed alive, glowing, bubbling, throbbing.

But maybe it was my imagination, because after all I was crying a little bit—drunks cry easy, you know—and there was nothing in the whole goddamn world that seemed to be right or in focus any more.

Not since Velda walked out.

I got out the brown-bagged bottle of whiskey from my trenchcoat pocket and I swigged some down before screwing the cap on and slipping it back in where its weight was a soothing presence clunking against my thigh.

She had been more than just my secretary. She was the other P.I. in Michael Hammer Investigations. Nobody was better at undercover work. But nobody was better at dressing up a drab outer office, either, behind a reception desk. Though she had no secretarial training when she arrived, her high school typing classes had proved enough, and she soon came up with a personal shorthand. Still, there were plenty who thought I'd hired her strictly for her looks.

…tall, lithe, with wide shoulders and full high breasts and a small waist that flared into generous hips, all curves and valleys and toned musculature with beautiful Hedy Lamarr-like features dominated by dark almond-shaped eyes, framed by shoulder-brushing pageboy hair so black it reflected like new patent leather…

But it was strictly business between us. Or it had been until I fell for her. And till she fell for me. Anyway, I *thought* she fell for me...

Only now Velda was gone, in her way, like the Big Man was gone, in his... except in a sense, in a crazy damn sense, she was right here with me, they *both* were, as I stared into machine-gunning rain washing away the red froth in the sand that was all that was left of Wade Manley.

Wade Manley, the head vice cop who had put me onto Velda. The Big Man who had come to me and said the Sterling girl was a burned-out case of an undercover vice cop who needed a job, needed a break, needed a friend.

I just need somebody to step up, Mike. Somebody like you.

And I'd stepped up.

I got the bottle out again and used it. Left it in my hand this time.

Because except for that bottle, I was all alone now.

No big beautiful black-haired partner of a doll to back me up and keep me sane. To hold in my arms when she was hurting and for her to do the same for me and to stand at my side unafraid, throwing .22 slugs at some bastard trying to kill us both. She'd done that more than once.

But she shouldn't have let me cross the employer-employee line into loving her, first teasing me, then tempting me, though I'd never even been to bed with her. I never loved a woman more, but I'd never had her, not in that way, that crucial, all-important way. I was saving that for when the promise that went with the ring I gave her last year finally got kept.

And she was saving all of that lushness, from the ripeness of her scarlet-rouged mouth to the high thrust of her breasts to the flatness of her muscular belly to those endless legs, legs that would wrap around me one day, saving herself for me, just for me, all for me.

Then one day she was gone.

And now, four fuzzy months later, there was no Big Man, either, was there? No big slob of a cop to go drinking with once a month, back when drinking was a pastime and not a full-time job. No big slob of an honest cop who thought stopping drug pushers outside schools was more important than providing security for some political bigwig. No more fat slob of a cop who wouldn't give in to the slimeballs running the numbers or the bookies bleeding the town, and no more sloppy S.O.B. of a cop who couldn't be scared off by murder, the threat or the deed. No… there was no cop like that at all anywhere in this City of Dreams.

City of Nightmares.

Wade Manley was very damn dead now, but even after the drumming rain had come and gone, his stain would remain on the sidewalk for all those to see who didn't like his breed of cop… a faded splash for all the lowlife punks to laugh at… and all the big boys way up in the penthouses to sneer at as an example of what happened when a dumb damn cop wouldn't play the game.

The cop in question was dead all right, and buried, his funeral just something else in the paper that I'd missed... but his faded smear on cement would be there for some time for all the cop haters to gloat over. No big man after all, they'd say—just another damn cop. Another damn dead cop. A fatso whose pay had been a measly $6200 a year, and so what if he's dead? Good riddance to a guy out to kill fun for other guys.

So in the cellars they smiled, and in the penthouses they grinned, while behind the doors that separated tenants from owners, they didn't merely smile... they laughed their foul heads off.

And here I was out on the street... a sloppy damn drunk, crying a little maybe, but not so gone with grief or sodden with sauce that I couldn't contemplate doing something about it.

As I stood there, under my coat in a leather spring-action sling was an Army Colt .45 automatic and I was taking a fat chance of blowing a hole in my hip because there was a round in the chamber and the hammer was back. Not such a good idea, some would say, under the best of circumstances. But with a snootful? What was I thinking? Was I an idiot?

Or maybe not really such a fat chance as that, and maybe it *was* a good idea, because from where I stood, everybody but me was an idiot now.

Grinning, I took another snort.

They were all out there on the other side of the rain laughing or waiting for some fool to try to do something about the Big

Man's death, and maybe they knew I was the Big Man's pal, and what that could mean for them, only maybe they heard that Mike Hammer was a drunk now and I was on my way to being an even bigger slob than the dead cop was, and if they got me first, the joke would be on me, their laughter justified, because I'd just be an item buried behind the funnies, the notorious trigger-happy P.I. whose luck finally ran out on him. Just another dead lush now.

Well, let them think that.

Like I said, they were all idiots.

Idiots who hated me or anyway hated who I used to be. Idiots who had killed the wrong cop this time.

I drank some more whiskey from the bottle in the paper bag. It felt warm going down and burned in the furnace of my belly.

"That was their mistake," I said to nobody, rain sluicing off the front of my hat. The sidewalk was a little wobbly. "The mistake that makes them idiots—this time they killed the wrong damn cop."

Because I didn't believe for a second that this was a mugging gone murderous. I didn't buy for an instant that the Big Man had just been out walking in this foul corner of the city. What, for the air? For that lovely river bouquet? No, Wade Manley was down here meeting somebody. Something was supposed to happen, and he was supposed to be part of it.

Only something else happened, and his death *was* it.

Whoever did this had entered a very exclusive club for a rarefied brand of son of a bitch—a worldwide select society of sick pricks. Because this killer was a very special kind of killer now, wasn't he? He was a cop killer and that marked him.

For weeks to come, every copper on the NYPD would be after this special killer. They would turn over every dirty rock in the city and shake out every rat's nest and turn this part of town inside out and upside down. They'd give it a damn good go.

But the trouble was, if Manley's brothers in blue didn't find that marked man within those first weeks, other crimes would demand attention. And witnesses and even some cops could always be bought off. Time and money could erase that mark.

Not with me it couldn't.

I had plenty of time and money enough.

When the rain let up, I was standing there staring at the streaky smear of rusty sand when the squad car eased up to the curb, catching a strobe of lightning as it did, and the old harness bull beside a punk-ass driver called over: "Hey, Mac—you okay there?"

After a second or two I looked at the car.

The bull yelled, "Didn't you *hear* me, bud?"

"I heard you," I told him.

"This is a rough area. You need to move along. Find someplace else to be."

I ignored him. The older cop said some words to the kid driving.

For ten seconds there was nothing but a grumbling sky, then the door of the police car snicked open and the driver got out. He was one of that new breed. All done up in a new unwrinkled uniform and wearing one of those cool expressions that the young ones try so hard to adopt. Too much Marlon Brando and James Dean. He came right up close, real sure of himself, big and tough and young.

But too young.

Aging drunks hate anybody sober and young.

The rookie cop said, too nasty, "Listen, buster, you heard the man. You need to move along or get rousted into the drunk tank."

He seemed to be hoping I'd get wise with him. His hands were all ready for it, fingers curled and ready to become fists. Maybe he wanted to show off for the older cop.

Evenly I said, "I'm not bothering anybody, kid. I'm just standing here on a sidewalk my taxes helped pay for."

No slurring. Maybe a little over-enunciated in that way drunks do trying to play down their condition.

The rookie's upper lip curled. "So... you're a smart guy."

There hadn't been anything at all wise-ass in my tone.

But I bristled and said, "Yeah, rookie, smart as hell. So goddamn smart I'll knock you on your skinny tail if you don't back off before nothing turns to something."

"Sarge," he called back to the bull he'd been chauffeuring. "This guy smells like a brewery... we better take him in."

But now he was sounding like maybe he needed some help doing that.

"You're so damn green," I said. And I leaned in and grinned at him. Breathed on him. "That's not brewery, pup. That's distillery."

Nostrils flared. "Last warning. Move along."

My grin turned sneery. "Get back in the car and buzz off, you little jerk. I'm busy here."

There wasn't much color left in his face. He was blister white and his face got pinched-looking, the cords in his neck standing out. Whatever he figured rousting a drunk would be like, this wasn't it—they taught him to do things by the book, but the problem was the book didn't quite cover me.

The older cop spoke out the rider's window of the cherry-topped vehicle.

"George…" the older cop began.

"I can handle this, Sarge." Hand on his billy now.

I said, "You think I won't splash you, 'cause you're a cop? You better learn to read a guy's mood better, sonny. You got one more chance. Blow while you can. Get out of here while this is still a funny story about this big-mouth asshole you ran into on duty who thought he was tough, but you just couldn't be bothered… understand?"

The young cop's left eye was twitching.

The older cop, a beefy one, was getting out of the car, saying, "Now, George…"

I said to the kid, "You figure me for a hood, then take me in. But if you think you're dealing with some rummy, guess again. Just put a hand on me and see what happens, laddie. You know?"

The young one was all set to throw one at me when the bull was at his side, touching his arm, saying softly, "Ask him for his ID, George. Do it the right way."

The rookie took a breath and the older cop's presence seemed to remind him that he too was a cop and that this kind of stuff needed to stay impersonal and official. The kid let the mad seep out of his face and held out his hand.

"Sir, your ID please?"

I grinned. "Sure. Glad to oblige."

I fingered out the small wallet and flipped it open. The driver's license was on one side and the P.I. ticket on the other. His eyes pinched near shut when he spotted the name. Those eyes got even tighter when he slipped out the folded ticket that said I could pack a gun.

"Are you carrying right now, sir?" he asked.

I nodded and opened the trenchcoat—the suit coat underneath was already open, the butt of the iron apparent under my left arm, showing the rookie just what he'd been messing with because he hadn't learned yet how to read a situation.

Or maybe how to read a mean-ass drunk.

The older cop took the wallet and he didn't register anything much. Just enough for me to pick up on.

He looked at me and amusement played on his lips. "You're somebody on our list, Mr. Hammer."

"The one that starts with 'S'?"

"No. The one that starts with 'C,' son. Captain Chambers wants to see you."

"That right? I'll be sure to drop by headquarters tomorrow and see how he's doing."

A big hard hand gripped my shoulder, the bull's smile not threatening but the fingers meaning business. *Just how Wade Manley would have handled it,* I thought.

"No, that won't do, Mr. Hammer. The captain said bring you around to his apartment. No matter what time."

"Oh. Well, okay then. I'll drive over there now. Thanks for your trouble, officers."

The older cop's smile was wide and toothy, but his eyes weren't smiling at all. "Mr. Hammer, you're damn near drunk on your ass. Why don't you let us drive you over there? So we don't have to arrest you for driving under the influence. Unless you have your heart set on a night in the drunk tank, and would maybe like to earn yourself a hefty fine."

"Since you asked polite," I said.

As the bull escorted me to the back seat, I glanced over at the rookie and said, "See, kid? That's how it's done."

CHAPTER TWO

Pat said, "How do you feel, Mike?"

I opened my eyes a little bit. It wasn't any harder than lifting a couple of concrete blocks.

"Nuts," I said.

His hand went up and nudged the shade of the standing lamp so the light wasn't in my face any more. He was sitting opposite me in a comfy chair, a drink in his fist, a tall glass coated with frost, and he raised it to his lips. There was an icy glass just like it on the end table beside me too, but I didn't want any. Against my head maybe, but not in my stomach.

This was the living room of Pat's apartment, a place I'd been many times but not lately. Nothing fancy—the kind of bachelor pad an upper-tier civil servant could afford. A window air conditioner was chugging. *Esquire* wouldn't be doing a photo-spread soon.

I was sitting toward the end of his nubby-upholstered couch. I didn't remember how I got here. Maybe a vague sense of those two uniformed cops, old and young, squeezed in on either side of me hauling me up two flights with the toes of my shoes thumping at every step.

"Whatever happened to that fabled Mike Hammer luck?" Pat asked.

He was in a sport shirt and chinos, looking more like a guy who wandered in from a backyard barbecue than a Captain of Homicide. A big young guy with all the talent in the world and trained to needle-point perfection in every trick and gimmick the department could think of. Brainy. Shrewd. He knew every angle there was and could figure out a few of his own.

"I ran out of luck a long time ago," I told him. My words hurt my throat trying to climb out.

"You did that all right."

He drank the drink half-way down, stared at the glass a moment, then set it on the coaster on the arm of the chair. He reached out and fiddled with the radio and stopped at Gerry Mulligan doing an easy "Stardust" and let it drift through the room.

I kept waiting for it but it didn't come. Any second now, I thought, and the lecture would begin. Cop talking to old friend. Cop with feet on the ground talking to guy with head in the gutter. First I'd get the serious look, or maybe the disgusted look, then the yak-yak. This time the floor would be all his. Before,

I had an answer for things, but not any more. When your life is one bottle after another, one slopshop after another, you don't have an answer for anything.

So I waited and nothing happened. Pat sat there stretched out, his head back against the chair, dreaming with the music. I forced a grin across my mouth but he didn't see it. The grin faded back to where it came from. Once he opened his eyes, seemed to look past me a second, then closed them again.

Damn it, what was he *waiting* for! If he was expecting me to groove out on modern jazz he should have known better! I was strictly a classical guy.

Oh, it took a while, but I got it. Pat wasn't waiting for anything. I could sit there or get up and go if I felt like it. Pat just didn't give a damn any more either.

The hollow place inside me got bigger. A guy always figures he's got one friend left no matter what happens. Everybody else could go jump, but he's always got that one friend. That's what I thought. Now it was different and it wasn't much fun coming back from the dead after all.

I stared at him and, almost as if he read my mind, his eyes came open. "Say it, Pat."

His hand went out for the glass. "How long has it been since I saw you, old buddy?"

"Four months maybe."

"Where you been keeping yourself?"

"Who knows? Here, there, everywhere."

"More like down, down, down. Going lower all the time."

I shrugged. "So what skin is it off your ass, Pat?"

The gray-blue eyes narrowed. *He was just pretending not to give a damn.* "Have you looked at yourself in a mirror lately?"

"I got better things to do."

"I bet you do."

"Who cares how I look? I know how I feel. Maybe I look the same as ever."

"Not hardly." The glass went up and he finished it off. He looked at it as though he was sorry to see it go before setting it down again.

"You're a lot of things, Mike," he said.

"I'm a versatile bastard."

"And you've *been* a lot of things. But this is the first time I ever made you for a sucker."

I could feel the red starting to creep up my neck. My hands were two balls that wanted to bust him in the teeth. "Shut up, Pat."

"Or what? You'll shut me up?" He didn't scare a bit. "Four months ago you could take me, kid. Right now I can say anything I feel like to you and the first time you get tough, I'll turn you inside out and sideways."

He wasn't kidding. Not even a little. His face wasn't smiling and he looked all nice and loose, the way a guy should be when trouble is in front of him. He wasn't all knotted up like me and his belly was flat under his belt, where I'd gone flabby. The eyes were clear and dangerous, but would stay friendly if I wanted it that way.

The mad that was inside me drained out and I

leaned back on the couch. "Okay, so I'm a sucker. So I'm getting soft."

"In the head, too."

"Why don't you lay off me."

"We used to be pretty good friends, Mike."

"Then lay off me."

He sat forward, the eyes tensed but not angry. "Not me, pal, I'm not laying off you. Maybe everybody else can keep out of your way, but not me."

Now I felt better. As long as there's one friend left, a guy always feels better.

"What was the idea," he said, "of giving those cops a hard time?"

"The young one gave me a pain."

"He'd have given you a pain, all right. You really think in your condition you could take a young buck like that?"

"On my worst day."

"Maybe on your best. If Sergeant Clancy hadn't been there to stop it, you'd be in Bellevue right now. Or in stir, if you'd got to that .45 of yours."

I said nothing.

"And what the hell's the idea of going around in this alcoholic haze with that rod, hammer-back, one-in-the-chamber? You really think shooting your own balls off is a good play?"

I patted my left side. The gun was gone. He nodded over to a table where it lay like a decorative touch.

"You can have it back when you go," he said.

I started to get up but my legs went wobbly.

Pat held up a hand. The gesture was gentle, not forceful. "Just sit back. We're going to talk."

I sat back, but I didn't talk.

"You been on a four-month bender, Mike. That's your privilege. I think you're on a collision course with getting dead—some barroom fight you lose all the way, or maybe your liver gives up the ghost. But that's your business."

"Damn well told."

"I been keeping track of you, pal. Oh, not messing in your business. Just put the word out to the boys on the street to let me know what's going on with you. They call them 'Hammer spottings.'"

"Cute."

"But a few days ago you dropped off the radar. Where you been, Mike?"

"Rio. I do out of town jobs sometimes."

"You don't do any jobs, not lately. You see, I expected you to turn up."

"That right?"

He nodded. "That's right. I expected to see you at the Big Man's funeral, but you didn't show. Maybe your good suit was in the cleaners."

I said nothing.

"I figured when Manley bought it, you might pull out of your stupor. Get some ideas about doing something about it."

I said nothing.

"Here's how I figure it, Mike. You were so far down your drunken rabbit hole, you didn't even know the Big Man was dead. Then somebody mentioned it to you, maybe in passing, and you crawled out and confirmed it and that's why you were down near the riverfront studying a certain patch of sidewalk tonight."

I said nothing.

"Something stirred in the back of that scrambled skull of yours, buddy. Some old juices got flowing. Even half in the bag you could look at the circumstances of the killing of Captain Wade Manley and know that the conventional thinking on the subject was horseshit. That was no mugging. He was down there for a reason. Somebody conned him down there and killed him. Am I on the mark?"

I said nothing.

The eyes tensed again and the friendliness was gone. "Well, you're not Mike Hammer anymore, get it? You're just a screwed-up drunk walking around inside his skin. You are no more ready or qualified to go on a kill hunt than the next Bowery bum."

"Somebody murdered him, Pat."

"I already said that. Pay attention. If you can. You need to go crawl back into the gutter, Mike, or check in for the cure someplace. You want the latter, I'll help. I'll be your best friend again. But if you go out in this… this feeble condition, looking for Manley's killer? I'll take you off the streets myself. For your own damn good."

He was breathing hard now.

"You through, buddy?" I asked.

He said nothing.

"So then who's going to get the bastard who did it, Pat?"

He swallowed. "I am."

"The by-the-book way? Or the other one?"

He said nothing.

"You know what 'other one' I mean," I said, and showed him the nasty grin. "The Mike Hammer way. The bullet in the guts and put a gun in the dead man's hand to make it self-defense way? Come on, Pat. Spill."

Again he swallowed. "I don't really know, Mike. I just know Wade Manley's murder needs a full investigation. Writing it off as a mugging gone wrong doesn't cut it."

I kept the nasty grin going. "No. No, I don't think that's it. You loved that old bastard. Like I did. You want the killer yourself. Maybe... maybe if I was in better shape, you could stand back and let me handle it. How would the shrinks put it? I'm the id and you're the ego or the superego or some crap? Hell, maybe I'm the super-id."

Very quietly he said, "I'm asking you as a friend, Mike. I'll give you whatever help you need right now to get yourself back on your feet. But leave this one to me. Please."

Damnit, he was right. I was in no shape to take one on. And maybe he *could* handle this one. By himself, backed up by the expertise and resources of the NYPD.

"*Could* you do it, Pat?"

"What?"

"Back a guy up against a wall and pump four into his guts and watch him die?"

"…I think I could."

"But could you *live* with it? Would you be killing Pat Chambers as much as the bastard who killed Manley?"

He said nothing.

"Better think it over, kiddo. Better think it through. Being Mike Hammer has its benefits." I gestured to myself. "But it has its costs, too."

Mulligan was playing "My Funny Valentine" now.

"Ever hear from Velda?" he asked.

It was a low blow and a sucker punch and I grabbed either side of the couch cushion beneath me and squeezed. Slowly. I didn't want him to see what was happening to me. I kicked the things in my mind back into the niches where I had stored them and clamped my teeth down hard to keep them there.

"Pat," I managed, "you can be a real sweetheart when you want to. Why don't you shut the hell up."

He laughed, a nasty hard laugh that was like a slap across the jaw. "Why is that such a sore subject, pal? It's just another dame, right? How many have you run through in your time, Mike? Some you use and throw away."

"I said shut up, Pat."

"Some you really go for, really fall head over heels for—how many of those have they had to bury because of you?"

"Pat…"

"You're a real he-man with the women. Even when one dies because of you, you come out of it twice as tough and nastier than ever and the babes think it's great. Hell, they love it. Love the big hero of the headlines."

"Enough, man."

"All but one. One who knows what you are and why you're like that and yet she loves you in spite of it. Or anyway she used to. *What happened to Velda, Mike?*"

"*Damn it, Pat, how the hell do I know!*"

I was tight as a bow string and my brain was a seething, squirming, nasty mess that wouldn't let me think.

I gasped, "Am I supposed to keep tabs on a dame every time she walks out on me?"

"Sucker," he said. "You're just a stupid sucker who can't even take his own damn advice." He pointed a finger. "She was the only decent thing that ever happened to you and you let her walk right out without even bothering to find out what happened."

I swallowed thickly. "Look… can it, Pat. I've had enough of this crap." I wiped my hand across my eyes and the sweat was warm and sticky. "She's a grown woman. She does what she pleases. If she wants to walk out, that's her business and I'm not worrying about it."

"No?" His grin was as caustic as lime. "Not much. For a guy who doesn't give a damn, you sure can make a wreck of your life in four months' time. Take a look at yourself, buddy, and see what's left. Look under the dirt and the beard and see what too much booze does to a guy. Go back and take a look at what the mice and spiders are up to in your office. That travel agency next to you put in a complaint."

"So what? I'm paid up six months in advance. The apartment, too."

"You're lucky you had some sense back when you were sober. That big insurance pay-off was a real windfall. Velda probably talked you into doing something smart for a change."

"Nuts."

"Yeah, yeah… nuts. That's a great answer. That's what all the bums say. Hell, that's *all* they can say, and brother, you're right there with them. You look right at home in a gutter."

I let go of the cushion and slumped back into the couch. All of a sudden I was tired. Too tired to bother reaching for an answer. Way too tired to argue with him, and pasting him one was a wish that I couldn't make come true. Anyway, he was right, wasn't he?

Pat's fingers were drumming against the fabric. He said, "I might have been able to help, you know."

I looked at him, then looked away.

"Four months. You never even bothered to stop by. I thought we were friends, Mike. What about it?"

"Sorry."

"That's all, just sorry?"

"Just… sorry."

"Well, it's not enough. Mike. What about Velda?"

I let the breath out of my lungs and reached for a cigarette. There was one crumpled Lucky left. When I straightened it out and got it in my mouth, the match I held up in front of it shook as if a wind were blowing from two directions at once.

The smoke felt good, though. Felt like it had been days since I'd had a good pull on a butt and I held it down deep to enjoy every bit of it.

"She's gone, Pat," I told him, through exhaling smoke. "I don't know where or why and you can't help any either."

Just that note. That terrible, so simple note in that lovely fluid hand: "*Mike—goodbye. V.*"

"You're still acting like a sucker," he said quietly.

My eyes half-way closed at the tone of his voice. "You're starting to sound like a cop, not a friend."

"I'm your friend, and I'm a cop, too. It seems to me that you were one guy who never played the cops down. You start forgetting that, like you did tonight with those two officers, and you'll never be the man you used to be."

He searched my face to see if I was still in there somewhere.

Then he got up and went to the little liquor cart and swished another drink into his glass. He didn't sit down this time. He stood right in the middle of the room balancing on his toes with a flat expression on his face like my old man used to have when he dragged me out to the woodshed for a waling.

"I said I could have helped, Mike, if you'd come to me first."

"How, Pat? She walked out, that's all. No questions, no explanations."

"Did you ever stop to ask yourself why?"

I dragged on the cigarette, avoiding his eyes, letting the smoke seep out my nose. *Mike—goodbye.* That didn't seem to require much interpretation.

"I guess I didn't," I admitted.

"Well, I *did.*"

My eyes asked him what he'd come up with.

"She had your ring, didn't she?"

I nodded. A sapphire. A sort of engagement ring.

Pat shrugged. "She wasn't the kind of dame who'd just pack up because of a fight or some dumb thing you did. The kind to leave without a word. Was she?"

"No." And there'd been no fight.

"So she left for a reason. She had to leave that sudden way, even though she knew you might be jerk enough to work yourself down to the gutter over it."

For a second he studied the ice as he swirled it around in the drink, then finished it all in one pull. "That's a hell of a funny thing for a girl to pull who's supposed to love a guy."

"That's what I thought too," I told him.

"Okay, then look at it a little while. Study it like a detective and not a big slob with his feelings hurt."

I pawed at the air and it took damn near everything out of me. "What's there to look at? Damn it, the thing's over with. Like you said, I'm a jerk. A sucker. Let it go at that."

"Right now you're a jerk all right… but there's room for improvement. You might even stop being a sucker."

The cigarette was starting to taste sour. I squashed it out in the ashtray on the end table and let it smolder. "What're you getting at, Pat?"

"You… and her. I'm interested because you're friends of mine. You and me go way back, clear to the Pacific. You ought to be thinking, man, not just beating your head against the wall. When you didn't show for weeks on end, I put out feelers and got wind of what happened."

"Great to have a friend."

"It sure is. Now… do you want to know where Velda is?"

I wanted to say no, but something wouldn't let me. I wanted to get the hell away from there but my feet were nailed to the floor. The burn started down low and worked its way up until my head was a boiling cauldron, spilling its poison over until my face twitched, leaving my teeth bared and my mouth dry.

"Yeah," I said. "Why don't you tell me?"

"While you've been getting plastered in this Bowery bar and the next one, she's been down in Miami somewhere, playing footsy with the lousiest punk this side of hell."

The heat all melted away. It fused my insides and dried them up. Where the heat had been was nothing but a sick, hollow space that echoed Pat's words briefly and gave way to the unearthly cold that comes with the grave. All the tension in my body slackened, the rage wiped off my face with one fast backhand of a remark that was worse than a club smashing my skull in.

Maybe it was better knowing than not. Maybe it was better to have it happen this way than to walk in on her sometime and see the beast with two backs.

"What's the score, Pat?"

"That's up to you to figure out, friend. I found out where she is, now it's up to you."

I made a sad attempt at a grin. "Not me—I'm out of her life now. Seems like she made it pretty definite."

"You might think so, but if you study the picture long enough, some very cute angles come in."

"Tell me about them, Pat. I'm in a mood for listening. Go ahead, tell me about me and Velda and all the cute angles."

He walked to the chair, turned it around and sat on the arm. His face still had that flat expression, his eyes trying to read things in my mind. He'd have to work at that. Whatever had been in my mind was gone now.

"Tell me," I repeated.

"You were two people in love. In fact, she had you right on the brink of taking the big jump."

"Wrong," I said. "*I* had me ready to make the jump. She never pushed me into anything."

"Because she loved you too much to do that.

Enough to take you on your own crazy terms. And you liked that about her."

"I did."

"Okay, then—for a guy who's ready to marry a girl, what did you know about her?"

"I knew she was lovely. I knew she was smart."

I remembered the first time she'd set foot in my office—tall, her hair black and curling down to her shoulders, those wide shoulders. Her black dress sported a low neckline before they even started making low necklines. Legs out of this world. Like she'd walked down off a calendar.

"And you knew she could qualify for a P.I. ticket," Pat said. "You have to serve in some police or government investigative service for at least three years at a rank higher than that of patrolman. And she'd been on the vice squad, right?"

Pat knew the story—that I'd come across Velda on the street with a big guy brutalizing her. I'd had no idea that she was an undercover officer trying to bring down a particularly brutal pimp. I happened along at just the right time and saved her from the bastard, who made the mistake of pulling down on me and died for his trouble. Funny. She'd been blonde then, hair dyed for the job. Hard to think of her that way now.

"Did you ever wonder why a woman like Velda went into police work," Pat mused aloud, "when she might have cracked modeling? Or even the movies? She was a natural for that."

"Also a natural for vice," I said. "What are you getting at, Pat?"

"Meeting you was strictly an accident. But maybe you fitted her purposes nicely. It gave her a chance to work under a new, perfect cover."

"Get to it, Pat."

"Nothing to get to. You just have all the luck even when you hire a secretary. If ever a P.I. could use a secretary who could back him up the hard way, Mike Hammer was it."

"You're saying she was, what? Still doing vice jobs on the side?"

"Maybe. But if she walked out when there'd been no trouble between you…"

"There wasn't."

"…and if she really was crazy enough to be crazy about you…"

"She was."

"…then for her to just up and leave, there must have been a damn good reason."

He was right. But what?

Pat sighed. "I'm all done talking, kid. I just wanted you to know where she was."

"All right. So now I know. Thanks a bunch."

I started to get up, but he stopped me with: "For the first time in your life, Mike, you're afraid to face something."

The way he said it was like getting doused with cold water.

"You wasted a lot of time," I said, half out of the chair. Dawn was working at the windows. "I don't know why you bothered."

"I bothered because Velda is a friend of mine… and I thought you were too. I bothered because the guy your girl ran off with is trouble."

I sat back down, hard. More like collapsed into the damn couch. "What the hell do you expect me to do? Go down there and drag her back? The hell with her!"

"Sucker."

"My ass! I'm not running after any dame, even Velda. What, and beg her to come home with me? Shit. If she wants to play around with some lousy son of a bitch, let her."

Pat's grin was damn near as nasty as anything I could serve up. "She may have been doing a little bit of playing around even before she dumped you, chum."

I was glad to take that one sitting down. It was one of those things no guy wants to hear. "Who the hell says so?"

"I'm a cop, remember? It isn't hard to back-check on somebody. If you're interested, I could tell you a lot of things."

"Don't bother. Maybe I wouldn't believe them."

"Not even the name of the guy? The one she hooked up with here, then ran off to Miami Beach with?"

"Stick the answer where the sun don't shine, pal."

"Oh, that was weak, Mike. Real weak." The grin turned into a wicked smile. "Hurts, doesn't it?"

"I said, stick it."

"Nolly Quinn."

"*What?*"

"Nolly Quinn, Mike. Remember him? Ran the poshest call girl ring in the city, after the war, till the reformers ran him out. Hell, he's been on the books in practically every state in the union and never once convicted. He's a slick, good-looking devil who knows his way around the dames and, brother, do they eat him up. His bankroll's fatter than your head. Money, looks, mob connections—that's a combination you can't easily beat these days."

"Where are you going with this, Pat? What is this, your idea of shock treatment?"

All sarcasm, all manipulation, left his voice and his manner. He was all cop as he said, "Four months ago, Velda leaves town, with no notice. A few weeks earlier, she makes contact with Nolly Quinn, in Manhattan on unspecified business. Two weeks ago, Velda's old boss— Captain Wade Manley, remember him?—dies under highly suspicious circumstances. Is there a connection?"

"Like what?"

"You tell me."

My head was throbbing like a hammered thumb. "What are you asking from me, Pat?"

"Nothing. But maybe this would be a good time for you to go down to Florida and dry out. And maybe look up your old girl friend and see what the hell is going on. She may not even know the Big Man is dead—it's not a story that would make the Miami papers."

I grinned at him. "You just want me out of the way. You want Manley's killer for yourself."

He grinned back. "Having you out of my hair during my investigation, let's just call it a side benefit. But this may be bigger than a dame running out on a guy and an old copper getting mugged and killed near the waterfront. And me working this end of it while you check out the Miami end might tell us what that big something is."

I made my mess of a head think about it. Then I said, "You got a contact for me down south, Pat?"

"Yeah. Captain Barney Pell of the Miami P.D. He's the one who spotted Velda down there." He had the slip of paper ready for me in his pocket, and handed it over.

I took it, then got up slowly. I reached for my deck of Luckies before remembering the pack was empty. The wrapper crumpled in my hand and dropped on the floor.

My voice was scratchy. "I'll think about it. Maybe I'll get sore enough to go down there and beat the crap out of Nolly Quinn on general principles."

Pat's laugh had a funny sound I wasn't familiar with. "Yeah, you do that, but first take that look in the mirror. Four months is a long time, my friend. You're sloppy. You got rust all over you. If you don't play it right, Quinn'll cut you in half the first time you move in on him."

I collected my .45 and made it to the door.

"Keep in touch, buddy," he said.

I went out and slammed the door shut. My feet

dragged me down the hall and I punched the button for the elevator. Something like urgency was building in me. I couldn't wait for the damn thing to get there; damnit, I didn't feel like waiting for anything.

In my mind, that beautiful face was looking at me and she was laughing and then she was crying and I wanted to smash something, anything, so damn hard it would bust in a million pieces.

My hand rolled up into a fist and I slammed it into the steel elevator doors again and again and again and then those dented doors slid shakily open and the operator inside was staring back at me with terrified eyes.

I stepped in with my hand streaming blood and said, "Take me down."

CHAPTER THREE

You can make it from Manhattan to Miami in a day if you are clear-headed, tireless and able to grab quick bites and bathroom breaks along the way. When you are coming off of four months of boozing, the trip takes four days. You won't even know the names of the towns where the cheap motels are where you keep showering to get the sweat and the stink off you, and the beds are just a this-one-sagging that-one-brick-hard blur of a rack where you can't sleep, you can't sleep, you cannot goddamn sleep, and when you finally do sleep, the nightmares come.

I'm back in that abandoned paint factory full of monsters in overcoats who have Velda strung up naked by her wrists, drooling creatures whipping her not for information but the sheer hell of it, only this time I don't have a tommy gun, I have only my hands and that isn't enough when they swarm me and take me apart joint by joint, flinging pieces of me over their shoulders in a shower of scarlet while my screaming makes a terrible harmony with the soprano wails of the flayed girl.

I'm walking down that street where the Big Man had been killed and it's raining, raining hard, gutters overflowing, and I'm alone, so alone, until behind me suddenly comes every son of a bitch I ever killed, charging at me with demented grins and guns and knives and axes and ropes and the dead beautiful women among them are naked but wielding fist-raised ice picks and there are Japs with machetes mingling with the mobsters and they swarm me, too, all of them.

Worst of all is the bar I go to where I start drinking again, drinking hard, shot after shot of straight rye, and Pat and Velda and Wade Manley and my old man and my dead mother, too, gather around me with sorry shameful expressions, shaking their heads while I try to explain myself between swallows for falling off the wagon again, and how I'll do better next time.

Bad as the nights are, the days are no better.

My hands shake on the steering wheel, like the car is trying to buck me off, though I barely go the limit. My eyes burn and my mouth is thick/dry and my muscles ache like they've taken a beating. Summer sun gets hotter and hotter. Twice a day I stop to buy new sport shirts and sometimes trousers, too—going to a laundromat doesn't cut it because the smell of me sweating out the booze into cotton is a stench that only a garbage can could love.

Yet I am hungry, so goddamn hungry, the furnace in my belly so used to burning booze it's demanding something, something, something, anything, and so breakfast and burgers and candy bars and beer (four times a day, strictly four times a day) go down and come back in tours of gas-station crappers where my screams of labor pain must scare off tourists and locals alike.

And thoughts of murder ride with me, as I crawl down highways with my mind and heart racing, smoking through three packs a day, daydreams of how I want that Nolly Quinn in my hands, where I can quell the shaking to squeeze and squeeze and squeeze his throat until his eyeballs bulge and I let go of him and he gasps in relief while those orbs still bulge and I dig them out of his face like clams in the sand and squeeze and pop and squish them like grapes and then the fun really begins…

Oh, I'd never hated anyone so much.

Imagine how much I'd hate him when we finally met.

It was hot, stinking hot as I finally crossed the state line, and the sweat leaked out of me until my shirt was a soggy mess that clung to my skin. When I stopped for gas maybe an hour out of Miami, I stripped off the sodden thing and threw it in a trash can and got a fresh one out of my suitcase from the back seat of the car.

The attendant, whose rolled-up long-sleeved uniform didn't look any fresher than the shirt I'd just tossed, grinned and eyed my plates. "New York, huh? Hell of a time of year to come to Florida, ain't it?"

"The next time I'll know better."

"How's things up there?"

Talking to humans was an effort, but I figured I better try to fit in. "Just as hot, not as humid. You from up that way too?"

"Yeah, Jersey. I shoulda stood there, too. But my old lady had a hunk of property down here, and figured we could develop it and sell out. Turns out nobody wants to buy."

"Business can't be that bad."

"It ain't. Business is pretty good, tell you the truth. It's only that nobody wants to buy. There ain't no other station around here for miles and that's why business is so good for gas, but it's also why there ain't nobody to buy the place."

My mouth was so damn dry. "You sell beer?"

"Sure. Inside. The old lady'll get it for you. Want me to check under the hood?"

I gave him the okay and went inside. Behind the counter, the nondescript woman in the two-dollar jumper reading the fashion magazine looked at me once, then without a word from either of us reached into the cooler and brought out a bottle of brew. I skidded a quarter across to her and used the church key that was already waiting.

Number two of the day. No more than one at a time for a month maybe, four-a-day total, and then it would be all right.

I looked at the beer foaming in the bottle, studied it until I knew every bubble by name, then shoved it between my teeth. My hand was shaking so bad, it was all I could do to keep from gulping it down like a thirsty dog at a millpond.

"You damned drunk," I said.

The woman looked up from her magazine, blinking. "What's that, mister?"

"Nothing. Sometimes I talk to myself."

"You're as bad as my husband." That had been neither nasty nor friendly—just a statement of fact. She went back to her magazine. I finished the bottle and set it on the counter.

The attendant came in wiping his hands on a paper towel. "That'll be a buck-ninety, bud. She took a quart of oil. Gave you the best, considering the ride."

The car was a beauty all right, a maroon Ford convertible with twin pipes and a black top, tucked away for now. It had been a gift from a Mafia admirer who felt bad for wrecking my previous heap, and among the hidden accessories had been six sticks of dynamite wired to the ignition and a back-up booby trap rigged to the speedometer.

"Keep it," I said, handing him two bucks and ending his speculation that I was a big spender. I went out to the car, climbed in, talking myself out of another beer. Funny how highway patrol guys frown at beer behind the wheel.

It was a little better driving. Not much, but a little. The smell of the ocean came in on the breeze, pleasant, but foreign to my New York nose. In front of me the heat bounced off the roadway and shimmered back to the sky. Back a few hundred miles, the trees and houses had changed shape and color, becoming unreal clusters of pastel stucco squatting under drooping palms. People were half-naked things hugging the shadows, whiter than you expected them to be. They knew to stay out of the sun. Nobody moved very fast. They were smarter than the city bunch.

Miami seemed to evolve out of the late haze of the day, first the sharp squares of the windows reflecting the red of the sun like bloodshot eyes, the shapes of the buildings forming around them slowly. Squadrons of gulls wheeled and dipped over the water, their cries strangely welcoming yet remote, like a butler introducing a guest to a party.

I unwound the handkerchief I had drying on the door handle and wiped the sweat from my face. Pieces of lint stuck to the four-day stubble of beard until I swore and brushed them off like insects. Up ahead a small rooftop neon sign blinked on and off in the blue dusk, the VACANCY as large and bright red as its name, SEA BREEZE MOTEL.

The motel itself was nothing special, just a low-slung one-story white clapboard with a two-story office midway, the end of the building painted pastel blue and boasting about both air conditioning and electric heat. I eased on the brakes and swung onto the gravel drive, following the U to its apex where a middle-aged couple sat in a yellow metal glider rocker outside the office. Only one car parked outside the dozen doors. Theirs, I suspected.

Still, crappy business or not, the man got up almost reluctantly. He was in a short-sleeve yellow-and-pink floral shirt and light yellow slacks, balding, in his forties. His wife was brunette and plumply attractive in a yellow-and-white sundress. She smiled pleasantly out of habit or duty or something. They were both working on bottles of Sun Drop sodas. They both wore sandals.

"Evening," the guy said. "Looking for a place?"

I nodded and climbed out of the car.

He grinned with ripe lips and big uneven teeth. He had a two-tier face, compact on top and jowly below, big nose and bright eyes. One of those ugly guys who come across friendly and even appealing.

"Well," he said, and gestured with both hands, "you can take your pick, mister. Off-season we're almost always empty."

"Too bad," I said. "Looks like a nice place."

That was an exaggeration, but not much of one.

"Oh, it's a swell little motel. We're full October through April. Matter of fact, we kind of like to see it empty after a busy season. Mother and me call it our summer vacation. Going to be staying long?"

"Maybe. A few days anyway. How far into the city?"

"Takes about fifteen minutes. If you want a swim, you can go right down here to the beach." He nodded his head toward the east. "Good places to eat up the road a bit," he added. He sneaked a quick glance toward his wife, who was engrossed in her soda pop, and winked and whispered, "You can find a real drink up there, too."

When he said the word my tongue snaked out over my lips. The breeze got suddenly too cool and the flesh crawled up my back.

"Yeah," I said. "I'll find my way around, thanks."

I followed him into the office and registered. With summer rates in effect, fifteen bucks bought me three nights. When he stuck the money in the drawer, he swung the register around, looked at it, and plucked a key off a board behind him.

"Glad to have you, Mr. Hammer. My name's Merle Duffy, but 'Duff' will do, and if there's anything you want just let me know. Guess you might as well take a shady-side cabin. It's a double and is more in season, but that don't matter none when the sun's this hot. Take your car around to twenty-four and I'll open it up for you."

The room was cooler than you'd expect. Duffy switched on the window air-conditioning unit and I could feel the temperature coming down to normal right away. The double bed had a light yellow chenille spread, the walls were light blue, the furniture gray. No TV. A few framed pictures of birds. It was a room perfect for a one-night stand or maybe killing yourself.

He showed me how to work the door, made sure I had plenty of nickels for the pop machine outside, then tested the running ice water tap in the bathroom to make sure everything was just right.

He said, "I think you'll like it better here than in a hotel in town. Much cooler and nobody ever bothers you. Cheaper, too."

Duffy didn't know it, but the not-being-bothered

part was the best reason for staying there.

I asked, "Anything special doing in town?"

"What was it you had in mind?"

"Oh, a little excitement."

"Tourist kind?"

I shook my head. "*You* know the kind."

His homely face broadened in a grin. "If you feel like tossing your dough down a drain, there's plenty of places for that. There's all kinds of fancy bars ready to sell you a drink for the price of a bottle."

I licked my lips the way a guy in the desert does when even the mirages don't come.

He was saying, "Nightspots right out of the movies, with big bands and top talent. Course, if after you've tossed your loot around, you might like to win some of it back, I hear they got some games open again. Some, anyway. I hear." He shrugged and looked dolefully in the general direction of his wife on the other side of the building. "Them things I don't know much about any more. Time was when I could take you there myself."

"I thought things were pretty hot in Miami."

His grin got sour. "I remember when it was a fun place to live. A guy could have his drinks and play his games."

"Yeah," I said. "The papers up north made it sound like the American Riviera."

"Papers did that down here too. Then that Kefauver character came along and everybody got riled up about it and raised a stink. So what good did it do? The place is still full of snakes with too much money."

"What kind of snakes?"

"Some of the biggest gangsters in this country live here at least part of the year, Mr. Hammer. Started a long time back with Capone." His eyes went over me carefully as if he were seeing me for the first time. "You some kind of cop or something?"

"Hell no." I made my face grin. "What makes you say that?"

"You kinda look like it. You sure aren't one of them sharp boys, even if that heap says you might be. Hell, even wheels like that wouldn't be good enough for that bunch. They all got foreign jobs or Caddies." He pulled the door open and stood there a moment. "Well, you want anything, just call, hear?"

"Sure, thanks a lot." I started to dig in my pocket for some change, but he held up a hand and shook his head.

"Mr. Hammer, I'm the owner, not the help. No tipping required. Just happy for a little male company."

"Thanks. And make it 'Mike.'"

He gave me another of those ugly, endearing grins. "Okay, Mike. If you live through whatever adventures you have tonight, you come give me a full report... outside of the little woman's earshot."

I laughed. First time in a while. "I'll do that, Duff."

I took my time getting unpacked. Down at the bottom of the suitcase was the .45 still in the sling. Some of the oil had oozed out staining a shirt with a greasy smear. I picked the holstered weapon up, dangled it from the harness, then dropped it in the top drawer of the dresser all by itself. I started to look up, saw myself in the mirror, and turned away.

Four months had made a difference, just like Pat said. A difference in how I looked, how I felt, even how I thought. The four days driving down here had worked out some of the poison. I was coming out of it. There would be no D.T.s or seizures or any of that fun stuff. Maybe I was getting my luck back.

But when I held my hand out and stared at it again, it still shook. You don't fool around with a rod when you get that far gone. The thirsty bastard in my head wanted a drink and I could feel the cotton working around inside my mouth. I swore out loud, stripped off my clothes and climbed under the shower.

I was going to hate it when I shaved.

It meant I had to look in the mirror.

The Herald Building was an old lady trying to stay young. The outside was all white brick and tile with oversize windows, but only when you were inside did you realize that here was part of the womb that helped give birth to the city so long ago. The furniture was antique, not deliberately so, but because it started life with this structure.

It was a wonder the elevators passed inspection. I stepped onto one and the uniformed gnome working the control said, "Where to?"

"City Desk."

"That's on four, sir." He pulled the outside door shut and started the car rattling upward. It was going to take a long time getting there. He grinned at me toothlessly. "Seems like most everybody uses the stairs these days."

I could see why.

At four, the car groaned, jerked and stopped. The operator motioned to the right with his thumb. "Just down the hall."

Up at this level it was a little cooler. Office doors swung open to let the night breeze pass through and the rattle of typewriters was like machine-gun fire. The *Herald* was a morning sheet and this was the time of its going to bed. I pushed through the gates into the city room, walked past the empty rows of desks to the rear where a hard-faced guy in a colorful sport shirt was correcting a proof.

"City editor in?" I looked reputable enough in my suit and hat and freshly shaved face to get away with it.

"Yeah, that's his cubbyhole over there. Ben Sauer." He pointed to a frosted-glass office taking up one corner of the room. "Knock before you go in. Gives him time to stash his bottle away. He doesn't like to get caught at it."

I don't want to see him using it either, I thought.

I said thanks and went back and knocked. Somebody moved inside the room, a desk drawer eased closed and a deep male voice called out, "Come on in."

He had been a big man once. The raw power of

a millhand stood out in the frame of his body, and life had gouged its lines deep into his horsey face, and taken most of the brown out of slightly too long, somewhat unkempt hair whose color was a sickly light yellow now. A long time ago somebody had broken his nose.

Looking past his size, he wasn't so big now. More like a fish that had been hooked and fought until it was tired. Life was trying to drag him up to the gaff, but only when you looked at his hands did you realize that though the fish was weary, there was power enough for one last, tremendous leap that could snap the leader and bring back the freedom.

"Ben Sauer?" I asked.

He leaned back in the chair, his eyes swimming a little bit. His white shirt had its sleeves rolled up and he wore red suspenders, a gray suit coat tossed on a newspaper-piled chair off to one side.

"I must be," he said good-naturedly. "That's what it says on the door." He frowned at me a little bit, trying to remember if he had seen me before. He decided he had, even if he couldn't remember where or when, like the song said, and he got chummy in that immediate way drunks do.

His grin was a loose thing. "You know what they call me out there?"

I shook my head.

"Whiskey Sauer." He pulled open that lower desk drawer. "Care for a belt? Despite the nickname, there's no mixer to go with it."

I shoved my hands in my pockets so he wouldn't see them jump. "No. Thanks."

Maybe I said it too loud. Maybe my face said more than my voice. His eyes came up from the half-opened drawer and ate into mine. "You've had enough already, huh?"

"I had plenty," I said.

"You look it, too. Sit down."

I did, taking the hardwood chair opposite him.

He asked, "Taking the cure?"

"My own version of it."

"Which is what?"

"Four beers a day and trying not to crawl out of my skin."

"Okay, so I won't torture you. The bottle stays in the drawer. You don't look like a man in the mood to socialize, anyway." He reached down and shut it. "You want something. What is it?"

"Information."

We were brothers of the bottle and he was ready to consider my request. "Well, a newspaper's the right place to come for that. I'm guessing you're after the stuff I can't get away with publishing, without getting sued or dead."

"That's about right."

The swimming eyes settled down some. "First tell me who the hell you are and why you want it." Then the humor came back into those eyes and he stretched out in the chair again, folding his hands behind his head.

It was my turn.

"The name is Mike Hammer. I'm a private investigator licensed in New York State. Down here from Manhattan."

A low whistle snaked out of his teeth. "I *thought* you looked familiar. I've run a couple features on you, man. You don't look so good now. Bender?"

I nodded.

"But now you're on a case?"

"Not exactly. I'm looking for a dame."

"Join the club. What makes this one special?"

"She's hanging out with Nolly Quinn."

The fish gave a start, an almost imperceptible signal that it was ready to thrash free from the hook, its eyes gleaming with a sudden hatred for the angler who had hooked it. Then as quickly as it came that gleam died away.

The editor got up, pulled out a pair of file drawers, extracted one folder each and sat down again. From the first he dumped a sheaf of news clippings and two typewritten sheets.

"This is all about you," he said. He scanned the stuff on his desk briefly. Some were New York papers, but Miami clips, too. I'd attracted attention. "You have a disturbing reputation, Mr. Hammer."

"So I hear. I earned it. And make it 'Mike.'"

"And make it 'Ben.'… You've killed men. Something of a… record number of men."

"None that didn't need it."

His big hands scooped the clippings together like a card dealer raking in for a new shuffle. When he had them back in the folder, he emptied out the other one. It was a lot fatter than my file. There were fewer clippings, but more of those typewritten sheets.

He asked, "You know this Nolly Quinn?"

"Heard of him."

"Well, guess what. He's bumped more guys than you have, friend."

"Not all my kills made the papers."

"Nor did his. You won't find it in type, but I know about it. The cops know about it, too, and so do a lot of people, but said people won't talk because a good number of them are dead, and the ones who *are* breathing don't want to join Nolly's list. He's quite a character. Right out of Damon Runyon by way of the Marquis de Sade. You two ought to get along famously."

I got out a deck of Luckies, fished one out and lit it up. "The hell with Nolly. I didn't come down after him."

"Oh… you're after the woman."

"That's right."

"If she's running with Nolly, you'll soon realize it's the same thing, Mike. He takes his women pretty seriously."

"So do I."

The editor looked at me steadily. The swimming in his eyes seemed to stop altogether. He dropped the sheets and leaned forward on the desk. "Do I get to hear the whole story? Strictly off the record."

"It isn't much," I said with a shrug. "I had a secretary.

She was a lot of woman and we were engaged, or so I thought. Four months ago, she took a powder. The latest I have on her is she was down here with Nolly. If it was only that, maybe I wouldn't mind... but it looks like the thing started before she left. The guy was fooling around with her in New York, when I thought she was mine, and that kind of crap I don't go for. Nobody's making me look like a sucker."

"Sounds like this woman did."

"Not even a woman. Not when I'm finished."

"What do you expect to do about it?"

I shrugged. "I don't rightly know, but I'm damn well going to find out why she went for that character and when I do, he's going to lose whatever it was about him that she liked."

He didn't need to know, even off the record, the part of this that had to do with the late Wade Manley.

Rocking in his chair a little, he said, "Then, what? She gets her tail paddled and dragged home by the hair?"

"Something like that. I haven't decided yet."

"Maybe some of your reputation isn't deserved, Mike."

"Yeah?"

"Yeah. Sounds like you don't know women as well as they say you do." He tapped the folder with a fingernail. "And you sure as hell don't know Nolly Quinn."

He pulled the drawer open and reached in for the bottle. It was out of habit, and he froze, his eyebrows coming up questioningly.

I said, "Go ahead, man. It doesn't bother me."

I was lying like hell and he knew it. My mouth felt dry and puckered and something in my brain screamed out to go ahead and get rid of the agony. One short one and everything would be smooth and in focus again. It would clear up the bells in my brain and take the tremor out of my fingers. I took another pull on the Lucky and looked away. If I couldn't get used to people drinking in front of me, I was finished.

The editor poured himself one, drank it down in two gulps, and said, "You got more guts than I have, Mike. I tried quitting once and got the D.T.s so bad they stuck me in a hospital."

"What happened?"

"They dried me out and my first stop upon my release was the nearest bar."

He corked the thing and put it back in the drawer, but the smell of it floated around the room, a tantalizing odor that clawed and scratched like a woman's nails. He sighed, wiped his mouth with the back of his hand and picked up a chewed cigar from the ashtray. "Now… what information did you want exactly?"

"Where I can find Nolly Quinn."

He nodded and slipped a pencil from his pocket and began scratching on a pad. It was half-filled before he finished and handed it across to me.

"There's a list of the places you might locate him. His home is in Miami Beach, where he also has a nightclub called Nolly Q's. But he's got a few legitimate businesses in town, a yacht in the basin, an office uptown and a few spots he seems partial to. If he isn't at any of those, you can ask around and find him. He isn't hiding."

"He should be." I folded the slip and stuck it in my wallet. "You said he has some legitimate businesses."

"Yeah. A few. Real estate mostly, a Miami staple. He's got a piece of a construction company. I imagine he figures to use them for a cushion if anything goes wrong with the other things."

"For instance?"

The editor let out an unintelligible grunt. "You name it, Mike. He's got his fingers in everything. Get to know some of the hundreds of flyboys you find hanging around here, then get them drunk and talking. You'll see what I mean."

"Smuggling?"

"That's the latest word. Nolly's suspected of being a big one in the narcotics business. He's said to have Mafia connections up your way, though we don't have enough to publish that. We know damn well he's got the fruit and vegetable business by the neck down here, but all the evidence the cops have on him, you can shove in your eye."

"What *about* the cops?"

"Hell, they can't move without evidence, you know that. They tried for years to clean this place up and when the feds stepped in, they did all right. Since that senate committee flap, the Miami area is strictly tourist."

"No illegal gambling at all?"

"The well-organized bookie ring that ran this town is gone. The strip joints are sanitized, the gay joints shuttered, drag acts illegal, bars close at two a.m. not sun-up. We've got legal gambling during the season with the ponies and dogs. There are a few protected spots, even a couple of outright casinos, but a relative handful. Nothing that will bring the feds back in. The Miami area got a real black eye from that, Mike. But this narcotics angle changes everything. It's big. And it doesn't run wide open and attract attention—we're just a damn port, a conduit."

"Cuba?"

"Highly likely. Like I said, you're going after a big one when you go after Nolly Quinn. I've heard it said that he doesn't use any of his gun hands when he wants a job done right. He takes any challenge to heart and cleans up the matter himself." He scowled at me. "Why don't you keep bastards like Quinn bottled up in their own backyards, and knock 'em off up there? Then the slimeballs wouldn't be down here making a mess of things."

"Don't blame us. I've done my share to rid the world of that breed. Anyway, you've got a few locals who've made themselves a name."

"Yeah, no denying that." He chewed on the stub of the cigar. "Miami attracts money and that's where the wolves gather. We're a playground for top gangsters, and maybe it's our own fault for letting them worm themselves so far in that they can't be shaken loose."

"Maybe you aren't trying hard enough."

"Think so? I wish I could show you some of what I wrote that got the spike. Hell, I could have broken the biggest local stories of the year, but when word got around, the pressure was put on the paper. They knew how to do it, too. They worked through the advertisers and scared 'em silly, and when the advertisers stop advertising we stop printing, so the stories never make the stands. Great, isn't it?"

"Things need changing."

The editor looked at me with a strange sadness in his eyes. "That they do, but it never happens. So. What about this girl friend of yours? What's her name, anyway?"

"Velda Sterling."

His eyes tensed, his mouth smiled slightly. "Tall, dark and beautiful?"

"Yeah," I said. "That's the one."

"Well, what do you know." He reached for the phone and held down a button on the base of the cradle. "Hello, Art? Look, get me some information on Nolly's latest window dressing." He paused, then: "That's the one. Right, right, address and anything else." He stuck the phone back in its rack. "He'll buzz me right back."

"Thanks, Ben. You're saving me a whole lot of legwork."

"Don't mention it. I'd like to see you and Nolly Quinn, uh… get to know each other."

"There'd be a story in it."

"That there would." He gave me the eyes again, up and down. "But I'm afraid if I put any money on the thing, it'd have to be on him. He's pretty fast with a piece."

"We talking dolls or guns?"

"Let's say guns."

"So he's fast. So am I."

But was I now? In this shape? Shaking so bad that I'd left my damn rod in a motel-room drawer?

The phone broke in with a sharp peal. The editor slipped the receiver against his ear and started jotting things down on a pad. He hung up, ripped the page loose and handed it to me.

"There you go. She's got an apartment in Miami Beach in one of the high-rent complexes. Art claims she's not being kept. She's strictly a mystery woman around town, seen on Nolly's arm but not moved in at his pad. She's got a lot of eyes on her, trying to figure the score, enjoying the view."

The slip went in my wallet with the other one. "Know anything about Nolly's friends? Associates?"

This time his grin had a sharp note in it. "Not much. But if you get anything, come back round and show your gratitude. I want to know everything about that guy, friend. Everything. When I get it all down in black and white, and can prove it? I'm going to dangle him by the short-and-curlies."

I snubbed the butt out in the ashtray on the desk and got to my feet. Outside someone was sweeping up and the building was vibrating from the presses rolling in the basement. My watch said a quarter after ten, but that wasn't important. Nothing was important any more. Looking at the time was just another meaningless habit.

I gave Ben Sauer my hand across the desk. He took it and I felt the latent power that still surged through him.

I said, "Thanks for the info. If I get anything, I'll call."

"Yeah, do keep in touch. You got my curiosity all aroused now. I feel like maybe I've helped shake things up a little. If there's anything I can do to help, let me know."

I said I would and I went out into the balmy night, thinking about Nolly Quinn.

When I found him, I'd find Velda, and I would see just what the hell was going on, and how the murder of Wade Manley fit in, if it fit in at all.

I went cold all over with the thought of seeing her again. Any other time, the thought of her would have sent warmth flooding through me. Now, I kept seeing her as she was, as she'd been, tall and lovely, something perfect and the only decent thing that ever happened in my life.

If Nolly Quinn had spoiled that, he was going to die slow and hard.

Even if I went with him.

CHAPTER FOUR

By one a.m., the life had left the city and the skeleton of it made a drowsy hum on the breeze that came in from the water. The streets were empty except for the occasional taxi or lost tourist and the smell of the exhaust from the air-conditioning units hanging heavily out of apartment windows lay a blanket of hothouse smells down the sidewalks. Across Biscayne Bay, Miami Beach would be alive and hopping, for off-season, anyway. Not Miami. Not by a long shot.

I reached the corner and stood there a minute, watching the prowl cars come and go in front of the precinct house down the block across the way. At least here was a part of the city I could call home, a building I could be familiar with, without ever having been inside it, a routine, a pattern that was as unchanging here as it was in New York and as much a part of me as an old pair of shoes.

I felt for the deck of Luckies in my pocket, took one out, straightened it and held a match to the tip. The flame was a mocking thing that did a crazy dance before it was whipped away in a breath of smoke and with that one drag my mouth felt like dry ashes. I swore silently at the whole silly business the Indians had conned Sir Walter Raleigh into and the pack of butts went into the gutter. To make it final my heel squashed them into a mess against the pavement as I crossed the street.

The desk sergeant wasn't around. The station house seemed dead. Two uniformed cops checking stolen plate numbers on a clipboard looked up when I came over and said, "Detective Bureau?"

One waved down the hall with his thumb, and they got back to it.

This time of night, this time of year, the Detective Bureau bullpen was not bustling. This was graveyard shift, eleven to seven, and only a couple of desks were filled by guys living on coffee and who hadn't given up cigarettes like I had. I didn't need to ask for help because one of a row of office doors had CAPTAIN B. PELL lettered on its frosted-glass pane.

I knocked, got a "Yeah," and opened the door and stuck my head in.

The anxious-looking cop inside was penciling notes on a report of some kind. He glanced up at me with a big grin that was not the usual kind of reception I got at police stations.

"Captain Pell?"

"Come on in! Come on in." He was beefy but not fat, in a short-sleeved white shirt with sweat circles and a loose necktie, his hair reddish-brown, his pleasant, blue-eyed, bulb-nosed face lightly freckled. He got up fast, pulled a chair out from the wall and pulled it in close to the front of his desk.

I said thanks, sat down and by that time he had an open box of Muriels under my nose.

He grinned at me like an affable madman. "Have a cigar."

I started to reach, then remembered. "No thanks. I recently quit."

"How's that going?"

"So far so good."

He closed the box and put it on a corner of the desk, then grinned at me some more. "Glad for a little company, bud. See, I'm having a baby."

"I bet your wife's helping."

He laughed, some nervousness in it. "Yeah, I guess she is." He glanced at his watch like the birth was scheduled. "Any minute now, I guess. You got any kids?"

I shook my head.

"Quite an experience. Gets a guy all rattled."

"How come you're not at the hospital?"

He put up both hands as if in surrender. "I was, all day today. Connie's been in labor since… Christ, hours and hours. I was going batty and the doctor said I should take a break. Hanging around a hospital gets to you.

That medicinal smell was making my stomach jump."

"Not sure it was the smell doing it. Going to work's your idea of a break?"

"Only place where maybe I'd be distracted a little. No kids, huh?"

"No kids."

"So you never been through this. This waiting is rough. It's not so bad if you got something to do, but when all you can do is wait, you get all shook up. It'll be different when it's over, I guess. This is my first."

"No kidding."

He gestured vaguely toward the street. "Squad car outside, waiting to take off soon as it happens. I'm five minutes away with the siren. Can't be too soon for me. So you're not married then?"

"That's right. I'm no help."

"Glad for the company, just the same. Gets pretty quiet at night. Something I can do for you? What precinct you from?"

"I'm not a cop exactly."

At first I thought he hadn't heard me or hadn't paid any attention, but I was wrong. His expression shifted and his eyes made a funny, brief bring-me-into focus squint and his voice was different as he said, "New York?"

I nodded.

"Pat Chambers' pal," he said softly, eyes half-lidded, nodding. "Mike Hammer."

"Right. But we had dealings, you and I."

"A teletype conversation about two years ago." All

business now. "Killer named Capper drifted up your way and you spotted him, collared him. He was extradited."

"And executed," I said pleasantly. "Down your way."

He loosened up a slow grin and leaned back in his chair. "So I guess I owe you one, Mr. Hammer."

"Not really. But maybe you owe Pat one. All I know is, he gave me your name as a police contact down here." I shifted in the hard chair. "Where do you know Pat from? You don't sound like a transplanted New Yorker."

He shook his head. "Strictly a Magic City boy. Pat I know from cop conventions. You *aren't* exactly a cop, are you? You're one of those crazy characters who *should* have been, though. What kept you out?"

I turned a hand over. "I was in for a while. Pat and me, we joined up about the same time. After the war."

His smile grew harder to read. "Did they throw you out, Mike, or did you quit?"

Since we seemed to be on a first-name basis now, I said, "Well, Barney, after I won a couple of commendations, they stuck me behind a desk and I walked."

"Why? All of us have to ride a desk from time to time."

"Too many rules. I hate rules. And I hate crooked politicos who make the rules for the crooked punks that live just inside them."

He grinned and unwrapped one of his own cigars. "That ain't the real reason, friend. Is it?"

I showed him some teeth. "There's better things for you to investigate than my mind... friend."

"Not at the moment there isn't." He lighted up the Muriel with multiple puffs. The smoke smelled foul to me. "From what I hear, you have a mind that could stand investigating... if not by somebody, by something. Like a crowbar maybe."

I put the teeth away. "We have a mutual friend, Barney. Let's play nice."

He rocked back. "That's kind of tough for me, Mike. Playing nice. See, I used to sit back and think about you, fella. Oh, you got a lot of national play, plenty of press coverage down here, too. I used to think you were what I *wanted* to be when I grew up... because you pitched a fast ball and made it do what you wanted it to and you called the score before you even started the game."

"What made you change your mind?"

"Well, maybe I *did* grow up," he said. Smoke gathered between us like a threatening cloud. "Maybe I grew up a few minutes ago when I took a real hard look at you. Seeing you now? Well. You see, I've read just about every single thing written about you, and now I feel like a sap for doing it. You're a real disappointment, Mike."

"What were you expecting?"

No grin at all now. "Not a guy who's been reading the labels on too many bottles. You been drying out, haven't you, friend? But it hasn't taken yet."

"Pat's been talking."

He shook his head real slow. "No. He didn't say a word about your... condition. He just asked me to consider helping you out if you needed it. I'm not sure I want to honor that request. What the hell happened to you, Mike?"

A woman.

Pell was saying, "All of a sudden I'm sorry I ever looked up to you, and ashamed for reading all those things about you and feeling things nobody but me ever knew about. You make me feel like a fool, Mike."

"Don't crucify yourself, Captain."

"I should. I should climb up there and let 'em start nailing. I was a damn fool for thinking your vigilante tactics were a decent means to an end when the system got clogged up." He grunted a laugh. "What a damn dope I was. Hell, there isn't anybody on any department in this country that wouldn't toss this whole private eye business out the window, if they had half a chance."

"I'm just one private eye, Barney. And I'm not even licensed in Miami."

He pointed the cigar at me. "A good thing to remember, Mike. No, I don't think I'm going to be helping you out while you're in my town. For some reason, Pat Chambers has a soft spot for you, in his head most likely. But I have a feeling I'm immune."

"Why don't you hear me out first?"

His grin came back and got bigger and wider and I never would have minded it a bit except that at the corners, it wasn't a grin. More like a slap in the teeth that said I was as rotten as Pat had told me I was.

He said, "You know what it was that kept you

out of the department, Mike? Not rules. Not the old army rebellion against superior authority. You're something that police departments don't like to have around. You're a *killer*, man." His mouth tightened and something funny happened to his eyes. "Or I should say, you *were*. Now you're a has-been. You're a drunk. You're a nothing, Mike. I'm sorry to say it, but I see all the signs and they're not new to me. You're a drunk without a bottle, aren't you?"

"Yeah," I said.

"And how's that going?"

"Like I said. So far so good."

"Do you have a gun on you?"

I opened my coat and let him have a good look at the empty place under my arm.

"Smart," he said.

Then he looked at me with contempt and laughed the same way.

He never should have laughed.

I got up. "That one you're allowed, Barney. That *one* laugh. That one I make you a present of, but don't laugh at me again. I'm a nothing, like you said, I'm a has-been, like you also said, but don't laugh. I just came off a drunk that was a mile wide and a mile high and let me tell you something, brother, let your wife die while she's having that kid of yours, and the bender you pitch? Man, it will be even wider and higher than mine, and when you're on it, when you're deep in it, maybe we'll meet up and then you can tell me what you told me just now, and see if you can make it stick while you're saying it into the mirror of some slimy bar along skid row. They do have a skid row in Miami, don't they? If not, you'll make one."

His eyes were wide and his face was white, but as I turned to go, he said, "Hammer... Mike. Come back. Sit down. Let me... let me hear you out."

I turned and his expression was neither that of expectant daddy nor contemptuous cop. He was just one human being looking at another with something like respect. Or anyway understanding.

I sat down in the chair again.

"You want some coffee, Mike?" he asked.

"I could use some. Milk and sugar if you got it."

He went out and his nervous energy brought him back quick with cups for both of us. I tried not to let my hand shake noticeably as I sipped some.

Affably, he said, "I've been through my share of java lately."

"Bet you have."

He took down a healthy swallow and his smile had nothing contemptuous in it at all. "So, Mike. What brings you to Miami?"

I told him about the so-called mugging murder of Captain Wade Manley.

"Pat is working the New York end," I said. "But I think the answer may be in Miami. And I think you know what else brought me to your town. After all, you're the one who spotted Velda down here and told Pat about it."

He nodded. "I knew her from the articles I read about you. And it's no surprise they'd run photos of a beauty like her. Anyway, she rated a sidebar or two on her own."

"But those write-ups never revealed her former status as an undercover vice cop. She worked for Manley, right after the war, and when she'd had it with working with vice, the Big Man recommended her to me. She made a perfect secretary and had her own P.I. ticket, thanks to her police background."

His cop eyes were searching my face. "She was more than that, wasn't she, Mike? You two were an item."

I just nodded. "You already know she's latched on to Nolly Quinn. Or maybe vice versa."

He sat forward and stubbed out the cigar. That freckled face had a softness that the hard blue eyes belied. "And you think your Velda may have a hidden agenda? Like maybe revenge for what happened to Captain Manley?"

I shrugged. "I'd like to think she left me in the lurch to bring Nolly Quinn down, but hell… she's been here four months, and Manley was only murdered a few weeks ago. That wasn't the spark."

"Then there must have been a fire going already," he said. "Still, the Manley murder could be related."

"Could be."

He folded his arms, his manner as casual as his eyes weren't. "What do you need from me, Mike?"

"Mostly just a friend on the Miami P.D. I'm here

to make waves, after all. I may need somebody to run interference with other cops, and I know you have a complicated structure down here, with the sheriff's office and Miami Beach department and all. I'm going to be bumping up against Nolly Quinn, and I hope to drag my straying secretary back home, so things could get ugly."

Those eyes were slits now. "After she's been with Quinn, you still want her?"

"Do you love your wife, Barney?"

"Of course I love my wife."

"Then shut up about it."

He got it. He knew.

I sat forward. "Barney, is there any way you can put through a temporary P.I. ticket and gun permit for me?"

He thought about it only a second before saying, "We've made that kind of arrangement with out-of-town investigators before. Usually it's taken care of long in advance, and I'll have to cut through some red tape and call in some markers, but… yes, Mike. I'm pretty sure I can do that. Where are you staying?"

I gave him that, he jotted it down, then I said, "I already got a decent rundown on Quinn from Ben Sauer over at the *Herald*. But if you have anything off the books to share, I'd appreciate it."

The cop rose and went to a file cabinet and came back with a file folder that he tossed in front of me. I thumbed through. No booking sheets or other official data. Just surveillance photos blown up to 8" by 10" like movie stills.

"Oliver Thomas Quinn, thirty-six," Pell said, "has no Florida arrests. Oh, he *should* have, if nothing else than for running a casino wide open at his nightclub in Miami Beach."

Nolly Quinn was tall and dark and handsome, with a nice smile and a cleft chin and an athletic build. He was Cary Grant with a Clark Gable mustache and George Raft eyes. In most of the photos, he was in a tuxedo and in almost all of them he had a babe on his arm. A succession of babes, including several bosomy blondes of the Marilyn Monroe variety, but also—in just two of the shots—a gorgeous, tall black-haired doll.

Velda.

He saw me lingering over the two photos in question and said, "She's a lovely woman. I hope you can haul her back home. Whether she really is another of Quinn's conquests, or is here for some other reason, it doesn't really matter. Either way, she's in danger."

I looked up sharply. "Why?"

He spread the photos out and pointed to one of Quinn with a blonde and another of him and a redhead.

"Two of his previous paramours turned up suspiciously dead," Pell said. "The redhead is Dotty Flynn, a hatcheck girl at his club. She killed herself, wrist-slash job in the tub, six months back. The blonde is Kim Carter, a singer at Quinn's club. Hit-and-run death, last year. First ruled a suicide, the second accidental if homicide by definition."

My neck was bristling. "Two deaths by girls with

the same place of employment run by the same boy friend? It stinks."

"To hell and high heaven. But we haven't proved anything otherwise."

"What, is he a goddamn Bluebeard? Kills them when he's finished with 'em?"

Pell raised an eyebrow. "No. He runs through these dames quick, a month to three months, then dumps them. Half a dozen in the last year and a half just went their own way. Several are working in the area as anything from waitresses to strippers. But these two... maybe they knew too much."

"What about?"

The other eyebrow raised to join its brother. "That's probably *why* they were bumped—so we wouldn't find out what these two girls knew." He shrugged. Sighed. "Who knows what they witnessed? We suspect Nolly Boy is involved in illegal narcotics smuggling, by boat and plane."

"Cuba?"

Pell nodded. "But if your Velda is down here on some mission of her own doing... like maybe one of these dead girls was her favorite cousin or something... she is exactly the damn type who would find out things worth getting killed over."

My fists were tight, nails digging into the flesh. I stared at Nolly Quinn's slick, handsome face and thought about ripping it off like a scab and revealing the bloody visage beneath.

"Mike... Mike, are you okay? You all right?"

"Yeah. Yeah." I shook a fist into fingers and picked up the coffee cup and drank some. Going cold already.

A young patrolman opened the door and stuck his head in, wearing a big goofy grin. "Captain Pell? The hospital called. Time."

Pell got to his feet, grinning back almost as goofily, and stuck a big paw out to me. I shook it. First time we'd shaken hands.

"Wish me luck," he said, and was grabbing his hat and slamming it on.

"You won't need it," I said.

"Everybody needs it," he said, his grin just slightly off-kilter now.

Then he was gone, and I was alone with my tepid coffee and two glossy photos of a beaming Velda in a low-cut gown on the arm of a slimy hoodlum named Nolly Quinn.

It was almost three a.m. when I got back to the motel. All the lights were out, even the neon sign off. The only illumination came from a hunk of moon and some stars spilled around up there, and the only sounds were the insistent lapping of waves and a breeze rustling through fronds. The night was warm but not hot, humid but not dank. A little sweaty and a lot sultry, like a belly dancer on her last set.

I left the Ford four slots down from my room, on the off chance somebody tailed me here, but before

I went inside, I found myself staring at the stand of palms and semi-tropical flower bushes that separated me from the ocean. I felt weak but not shaky, and I craved neither a drink nor a cigarette. I'd had so many smokes coming down from Manhattan that my throat burned and my mouth had tired of the taste, and no real nicotine need had asserted itself since I tossed my Luckies in the gutter. At least not yet.

I might have been on that island in the Pacific where a tropical paradise had turned into a surreal hell, death all around me, buddies torn apart by bullets, ripped to shit by shrapnel, blown apart by grenades, vaporized by shelling, my M-1 barrel glowing orange-hot from all the fire I was laying down, my first kills distant, like carnival targets going down, but soon carnage was close range, where I could see and hear and smell them, the fear and hate in their faces reflecting my own, and we called them yellow bastards but they bled the same red we did.

I moved through the stand of palms slowly, ears perked for snipers, and half-way through I wanted to turn and retreat to that motel and my room and my bed and away from this memory-turned-reality.

But I trudged on through, and then the beach was there, its stretch of gold turned ivory by moonlight, the surf foamy and steady but gentle. Lulling. I looked left. I looked right. Either direction there was nothing and nobody at all, not on the beach anyway, though the lights of the city were a smeary distant haze. The water called to me in throaty tones and I got out of my suit coat and dropped it to the gently sloping sand

and walked some more before pausing to step out of the pants and pull off my socks. Then I began to walk again, toward the dark white-capped water, dropping the rest of my clothes like breadcrumbs as I went.

The night was warm like the sand under my bare feet, but the water wasn't, and the bracing rush of it nearly woke me from my semi-sleepwalker state. But not all the way. I walked on, right into the water, like Moses expecting the Red Sea to part, only it didn't, instead rising to my waist, then my chin, until finally I swam out a ways, working against the tide.

How far out I got I couldn't tell you. I reached a point where if I went any farther, I couldn't be sure in my weakened condition I could make it back. Treading water a while, I took in the wet black vastness around me and the beach and the palm trees and also a sky that made even the ocean seem pitifully finite.

Don't, Mike, Velda said. *Don't even think about it...*

I swam back, easily, steadily, in no hurry. I emerged from the water as naked as the day I was born but with plenty of scars to prove that I had been. I felt better. I wasn't shaking at all. The best part was I felt tired, the kind of tired that tells you sleep will come easy.

I gathered my clothes and, without getting back in them, walked swiftly through the tropical mini-jungle that separated me from a bed that called to me now the way the ocean had.

I went inside and dove in.

CHAPTER FIVE

I woke up with sun at the windows and came around slowly enough to know I'd slept a good long while. My wristwatch on the nightstand said it was nearly four o'clock—almost twelve hours.

I sat up and drank in fresh sea-tinged air—before I hit the rack, I'd shut off the air conditioner and opened some windows. Despite my grogginess after so much sleep, I knew something had changed. When I stretched, it didn't hurt so much. My mouth was thick with sleep, not cottony from lack of booze. I didn't even seem to crave a cigarette. And I wanted breakfast, not a beer.

My shower went on a good fifteen minutes. I started it out steamy hot and wound up letting icy needles have at me. After I'd toweled off, the damnedest thing happened: the face in the mirror was me. My hands were steady as I shaved, the first time in a long while Mr. Gillette hadn't tried to cut my throat.

I went to the closet where the clothing bag was hanging and selected the lighter weight of the two remaining suits I'd brought. Yesterday's was sandy and rumpled and abandoned on a chair like a skin a snake crawled out of. Before I put on the coat, I climbed into the shoulder sling, as if it were no big deal at all. I got the little can of oil from my duffel and shot a few drops into the .45's slide mechanism and checked the clip. Satisfied, I used a washcloth to wipe the gun off before I slipped it into the holster. The suit was custom-cut and concealed it nicely.

With that familiar extra weight under my left arm, I felt whole again. Complete. I was straightening my tie in the dresser mirror with the confidence of a human being when somebody knocked.

I reached for the rod but then the motel manager's friendly voice came through the wood: "It's Duff, Mike! Envelope came for you… You okay in there?"

Leaving the .45 in its cradle, I went to the door and opened it. Duffy's jowly, thick-lipped, bright-eyed puss beamed at me. The sun behind him made the fuzz on his balding head glow like a halo. He was in a pale yellow sport shirt and darker yellow trousers with the usual sandals.

"I was gettin' worried about you, Mike. Here."

He handed me a manila envelope. I motioned him in and stepped away to open the thing up. New baby or not, Captain Barney Pell had come through: I was looking at two white cards, each with TEMPORARY stamped on them and my basic information typed in. One was a gun permit for Dade County, the other a P.I. ticket for the state of Florida. I slipped them in my wallet.

"You know who delivered that?" Duffy asked.

"A cop in a squad car."

He goggled at me. "How the hell did you know that?"

"Educated guess. Has anybody else been asking about me?"

"No, Mike." He gestured vaguely. "Listen, usually the wife changes the towels and sheets and stuff in the morning, but with your car here, we figured we better not bother you. Even without the do-not-disturb on."

"Thanks, Duff."

"You going out? You want Martha to tidy up in here?"

"Naw. I haven't had a woman make my bed for me since I went in the service. Fresh towels and soap tomorrow morning would be swell."

Duff nodded. "Sure thing. You... look different."

"I feel pretty good today. I've been coming off a bender. Haven't had anything stronger than a beer in five days. Stopped smoking, too."

He grinned lopsidedly. "You do look better. But best be careful, feller."

"Yeah?"

The homely mug grew grave. "I come through my share of toots and let me tell you, after you sweat and piss and shit the poison out, you get on this kind of… hopped-up high. Like you're sailin'. Like the sun is shinin' out of your backside. It don't last."

"Thanks, Duff." Smiling, I put a hand on his shoulder. "I appreciate that. But I'm not an alky. I didn't fall off the wagon. A woman sent me spiraling. The booze isn't the disease. It's a symptom I thought was a cure."

"You know better now, huh?"

"I know better. I *am* better."

The motel manager drifted toward the door, paused when his hand hit the knob. "How'd your night on the town go? If you don't mind my askin'."

"I don't mind. I never quite got around to it. Handled some business affairs instead. But I'm thinking about trying Nolly Q's in Miami Beach tonight."

The ugly face frowned, not doing itself any favors. "I don't know, Mike. I hear a gangster runs that place, and it's got a reputation as a clip joint. A fabulous one, but a clip joint."

"I'm a big boy. I'll take my chances. Where can I get a decent steak?"

That turned out to be a boxcar diner on the way to Miami. They served breakfast all day and all night, so I had a rare steak and scrambled eggs and American fries. I was hungrier than a lumberjack on pay day. Seemed like food was my only craving right now. My stomach must have been starved for calories that didn't come from fermented grain.

The day was so sunny and clear and bright I stopped to buy sunglasses. The top on the maroon Ford was down as I rolled through little communities of cottages and haciendas, bungalows and trailer camps, all nestled in stands of palms and tropical flora that didn't give a damn what kind of money you had.

Miami itself was a different story, looking like what Manhattan might have been if Hollywood were in charge. I was soon in light traffic traveling briskly down four-lane Biscayne Boulevard where handsome older residences quickly gave way to white and buff skyscrapers. The Seventy-ninth Street Causeway took me across the blue shimmer that was Biscayne Bay, its docks given over to fishing and excursion boats, its roomy harbor home to private craft from houseboats to yachts. Before long I was cutting down Miami Beach's main stem, Collins Avenue, which ran the length of the island, hugging the stretch of golden sand.

Miami Beach claimed to be a separate city from Miami and had the local government to back it up. But how could a place with no manufacturing, no commerce, no slums, no railroad, no airport, call itself a city? It did have schools and churches and hospitals, and golf courses and parks. But mostly it was five miles of oceanfront hotels, ritzy nightspots, and swanky shops, all catering to the wealthy who flocked there in winter.

Right now its opulent white hotels might have

been the towering vestiges of an ancient civilization, attended by archeologists making a trek to some distant land, not tourists enjoying off-season rates. At a modest six stories, the narrow white apartment building just half a block off the main stem might have been a toolshed for one of the nearby white monoliths. A geometric slab bore the street number and held in place a marquee-style overhang around which curved the words WINTER HARBOR.

The building had a nautical look down to its oversize porthole windows. There was no doorman, but security wasn't entirely lax, because you still had to get buzzed through the vestibule. I only had to try seven of the twenty-four buttons before I got the only kind of buzzer that says you've just won something.

I pushed through double glass-and-steel doors into a pink-walled air-conditioned lobby with an ocean liner feel, thanks in part to its metal-banistered stairway and the life buoy design in the terrazzo floor. This pastel cavern I had all to myself—even the elevator was self-service.

One of the vestibule buttons I hadn't pushed was 504, labeled V. S. But I already knew that was Velda's number, thanks to Ben Sauer at the *Herald*. I went up to five and quickly determined there were four good-sized apartments per floor. Even the hallway was air-conditioned, its walls a light pink, the floor gray slate.

Velda didn't have the money or the attitude to stay in a place this posh. According to Sauer, she wasn't being kept, but the evidence said otherwise.

Like the lobby, the curving hallway was empty. This was late afternoon but there were no sounds of TV or smells of cooking. Maybe the residents were too high-class for something as plebeian as television, much less cook for themselves. On the other hand, I figured the apartments were mostly unoccupied off-season.

I stopped at 504 and rang the bell twice and knocked several times, but nobody seemed at home.

From my wallet I withdrew from their hiding place a small pair of lock picks. My hands were steadier than they'd been for a long time, but it still took ten seconds instead of the usual five to crack the new-model Yale number.

I stepped inside and called, "Velda? *Velda!*"

Nothing.

I almost tripped over the two suitcases just inside the door. Seeing the familiar copper-brown leather bags confirmed this as Velda's apartment, and made my stomach clench like a fist, as if I'd caught her with that bastard Quinn. I hefted the bags and found them heavy. Going on a trip? Moving out, maybe? *Already gone?*

But the fragrance of her was still here. Not perfume. That special scented soap she used...

Otherwise the pad didn't speak of her at all. Not that it wasn't classy with its light pink walls and light gray carpeting with darker pink streaks. Modern yet comfortable-looking furnishings included a pale pink sofa with red pillows, a low-slung white marble-topped coffee table, brass-based lamps, a dark rose chair with feminine lines. The floor-to-ceiling windows were sheerly curtained, and the framed pictures on the wall were pretty fair Jackson Pollock imitations.

Carefully decorated digs, yes. But not by Velda's hand. For one thing, she didn't like the *real* Pollock. She'd hang *him* on the wall before one of those kicked-over-paint-can paintings of his.

The living room was sunken with a kitchen off to one side. You went up three steps to get to the other rooms, including the bedroom. The scent of her was even stronger in there, though again nothing spoke of the woman herself. The walls were off-white, the carpet buff, the furnishings modern in the way of an expensive hotel. The double bed had a pink satin spread with a row of red satin pillows.

My eyes fixed themselves on that bed.

My hand twitched and rose to my chest and my fingers drifted inside my suit coat and then I was gripping the butt of the rod. It came half-way out like a beast from its cave after a twig snapped. I thought about shooting that goddamn bed and those goddamn pillows until the air was full of cordite and stuffing and sprung springs and goose feathers.

Then I eased the beast back into its cave.

The closet was empty and so were the dresser drawers. An adjacent bathroom was devoid of her personal articles. Those suitcases didn't represent a trip she was taking—she had moved out. Or anyway was moving out.

What did that mean?

Was she heading back to Manhattan to beg her way back into my good graces? A voice in my head said, *Fat chance.* Or was she moving in with Nolly Quinn? The voice said, *Now you've got it...*

In the living room, near the front door, I tried the suitcases and they weren't locked. I opened them one at a time and went through them. I didn't know what I was looking for. I told myself I was searching for clues. What I was probably doing was feeling the fabrics she wore, the jersey, the silk, the cotton. Smelling her. Touching her by proxy.

A small zippered area gave up a copy of *Quick*, a little mini-magazine with a picture of Janet Leigh in a swimsuit on the cover. Absently I thumbed the pages and caught the stiffer edge of a photo. I pulled it out.

It was a snapshot-size print of the two of us smiling at the camera, toasting the photographer, maybe with a little buzz on. One of those photos some doll takes at your table and if you like how it comes out, you buy a copy. I didn't remember ever buying the thing, so Velda must have.

Something warm flowed through me. Something like hope. Something that wasn't hurt or hate. *She had still cared enough about me to bring this photo along and hide it away. To risk her new boy friend finding it and belting her one over it.*

They came in talking and for a fraction of a second I saw them first—two big well-tanned crew-cut guys in expensive suits with the kind of shoulders that made pads superfluous. The one in front was so blond he was almost albino with light blue movie-star eyes and an ex-pug's battered mug. The one in back had bristly black hair and heavy black eyebrows over dark, close-set eyes under a shelf of forehead that gave him a caveman look.

That fraction of a second got me half-way to my feet before the near-albino rushed me. No discussion. No queries. Nobody caring why I was here or what I was doing, just that I didn't belong, and in a flash I knew this was not Velda's pad but the digs Nolly Quinn provided whoever his current flame was.

I managed a toreador side step and shoved the bull-necked blond skidding to the floor on his face, the carpet cushioning him some but not much. Then the black-crew-cut caveman was rushing me, and I thought about yanking the .45 out and slapping him with it, only once a gun came into play things could get out of hand, especially since I had no doubt these boys were packing, even if their suits were linen custom-cut numbers like mine.

I gripped the handle of the bigger of the two suitcases and swung it at the caveman, clipping him on the chin, sending him windmilling back against a wall and sitting him on his ass. While he was dazed, I dropped the suitcase and went over fast and grabbed him by an ear with one hand and hugged the shelf of his forehead with the other and smashed his skull into the wall until his eyes rolled back white and he slumped unconscious under the mini-Pollock he'd made.

The near-albino was getting noisily to his feet behind me and I swung around and charged *him* this time, tackling the bastard, taking him across the living room, his feet doing a stupid dance as they tried to find purchase until my weight made him lose balance and brought him down, his head hitting the edge of the marble coffee table. He went limp and fell over to one side, the back of his head wet with blood. But he was breathing.

So was I, sucking air in and letting it out, ragged wind as erratic as a short circuit, my heart beating fast, my head spinning a little. I was in no shape for this, and I either needed to kill these sons of bitches while I still could or else get the hell out before they came around.

I got the hell out.

Miami Beach was brighter by night than by day, and busier. The plush white hotels of Collins Avenue dolled themselves up with brilliant, multi-colored lights that bathed them in blue and pink and purple and green, casting a dizzying aurora borealis into the dark sky. Even off-season, the stem was alive with gussied-up tourists showing off their finest vacation wear and their brand-new sunburns. The retirement types had near-black tans and garish casual attire, parking themselves in beach chairs outside their hotels, watching younger and prettier generations parade by on their way to nightclubs luring them with a gaudy neon siren's song.

If the Winter Haven apartment house had been an ocean liner, then the nightclub just west of Collins Avenue on Twenty-second Street was an iceberg, a big block of white with pink and green trim and NOLLY Q'S in pink script neon filling a fourth of the facade. The windows were glass-block, letting light in but keeping the unpaying out, with a dark pink canopy and matching carpeted steps up into the joint.

Several well-dressed couples were going in when I came around from the self-park lot in back. The place seemed to be doing okay for this time of year, but I quickly realized I might be under-dressed. I was standing on the sidewalk staring at the place, like a kid considering an outfield-fence climb, when I felt a gentle hand on my arm and heard a tentative feminine voice say, "Excuse me… excuse me?"

I turned to see a delicate doll in a green satin gown and a mane of hair a shade of red unknown in nature but fine by me. Her face was heart-shaped, her lips thin but beautifully formed and moistly scarlet, her eyes as green as her gown. Her make-up was light, expertly applied. She was slender but in an appealing, long-limbed model manner that made her seem taller than she was.

"No apologies necessary, honey," I said, grinning at her.

"I don't mean to sound rude," she said, her voice an unlikely but fetching combo of little girl and worldly, "but are you alone tonight?"

I shouldn't have been surprised to find a hooker in her league working outside a high-priced joint like this. I kept my grin friendly as I lifted her hand from my arm like a butterfly I intended to let go.

"Sorry, baby," I said, "that's not how I play. Thanks, though."

She flushed in embarrassment. "Oh, this isn't a pick-up! I just need to go in the club, and they don't allow in unescorted females. There's somebody I need to see, somebody I simply *must*... could you walk me in?"

Desperation throbbed in her voice and in the almond-shaped, long-lashed green eyes.

"Love-life problems, doll?"

She swallowed and nodded, chin crinkling.

"I know the feeling." I glanced at the club, thought about my own situation. "How about we go in together and then take a table for a while? No come-on, kid. I just need to blend in better than some rube out on the town solo."

She nodded and smiled. It had a nice pixie-ish quality.

I held out my arm and she took it. Maybe the Hammer luck was making a comeback. This was not the kind of fluff a bum just in off a bender, adrift in a strange town, usually rated. Particularly without paying.

We went in and I checked my hat. I tipped the

maître d' a buck and he walked us to a table toward the front off to one side. The interior was what the suckers took for class these days—linen tablecloths, red carpet, mirrored walls, glass stage. A dance band in white jackets up on the latter was playing a rhumba. About half the male patrons out on the dance floor were in tuxes and all their dates were in gowns. I was under-dressed, all right.

"You smell good, sugar," I said, as I held out the chair for her at our table for two.

"It's 'My Sin,'" she said, and this time there wasn't any impishness about it.

"Well, it's a good sin to have," I said and got seated. "I'm Mike. Mike Hammer. Down here from New York."

She leaned forward. The gown had some neckline but she didn't have much in the way of breastworks. What the hell—I was a leg man anyway.

"I'm Erin," she said. "Erin Valen. Vacationing, Mike?"

"More like a business trip. What do you do for a living, Erin?"

"A little modeling. Some acting, some dancing. Waitressing, if I get desperate. I was in the chorus line here, till just a month or so ago. They don't bring in name acts off-season. No floor show now, just dance bands."

The place seemed fairly full, but a close look revealed landscape enough for twice as many tables. During the winter months, there would be.

"Not surprised you're a model, Erin. You're a natural

beauty. And that's no come-on either."

She touched the emerald ribbon at her throat and seemed to hold back a blush. "What do you do for a living, Mike?"

"Insurance investigator," I said. Not a lie. Just a reduction of the truth. "Have you eaten?"

"I'm not hungry. But go ahead if—"

"No, I ate earlier. Let's get something to drink."

She had a champagne cocktail and I ordered a beer, which rated me a patronizing look from the waiter. Apparently he wasn't interested in a tip.

I said to her, "There's gambling here, I understand."

"Yes," she said, and nodded toward the curtained wall nearby. "We can go back there if you like… in a while."

"We'll see. Full casino set-up?"

"Oh, yes. Everything you could want, slots to roulette. As big as this room. Bigger. The only casino in Miami Beach right now."

"The guy who runs the place," I said, "must know what wheels to grease."

She nodded, but her nostrils and eyes flared. I wondered if I'd touched a raw nerve. She got into her little green purse for a cigarette case, got a smoke out and looked to me for a light.

"Sorry, honey," I said. "I quit."

She dug in her purse some more and found some matches. Lighting up, she said, "Must be hard for you being in here. With all this smoke."

"Nah. Actually just makes me kind of sick."

"Oh! I'm sorry…" She was about to put the cigarette out but I stopped her, gripping her easily by the wrist.

"Doesn't bother me that much," I assured her. "And if it did, it's something I better start getting used to."

Our drinks came and we flirted a little as she told me about things to do and see while I was in town, and what not to bother doing and seeing. She had a bubbly personality that never crossed over into dumb-broad giddiness. In fact, despite the banality of our conversation, it was clear she was one smart cookie.

I took her out on the dance floor for a slow Latin number, "Perfidia," that the dance band's girl singer was singing in a sultry, romantic Spanish. That was when I spotted them.

Velda and Nolly Quinn.

They were at a ringside table and he was holding her hand while she gazed at him in apparent contentment. The reflective sheen of Velda's black hair was like a rain-slick street at midnight. It went well with the midnight-blue satin dress that left her creamy shoulders bare, touched by a Miami tan, the round ripeness of her breasts all but spilling out like fruit from a tipped cart. Her dark eyes were on him, that lush mouth smiling just a shade. She was everything the delicate creature in my arms was not—big, bold, brashly female.

And then there was the bastard holding her hand.

He was handsome, all right, and big, every bit as big as me, and in the flesh the Cary Grant resemblance was striking. The thin mustache might be a lame try for sophistication, but those hooded eyes told the real story—he came from the streets, where the only guys who wore tuxedos were lucky stiffs who landed jobs as waiters.

He was smoking, but not just smoking, that wasn't nearly good enough—he was using a goddamn cigarette holder. Christ, the son of a bitch could stand killing for that alone.

Erin said, "Isn't she a lovely woman."

"Yeah. Who is she?"

"She's Nolly Quinn's girl. That's Nolly Quinn with her."

"The guy with his name outside in neon."

She smiled up at me just a little. "That's right. You seem… are you all right, Mike?"

"Let's sit the rest of this one out, okay, kid?"

We went back to our little table. I ordered her another champagne cocktail, but I was still nursing my beer. It was only my second of the day, but the rule was never two at the same time.

She was telling me how boring modeling work could be when I noticed Quinn threading through the tables, pausing briefly along the way to nod and exchange pleasantries with patrons. He had a raffish smile and oozed charm like pus from a boil.

Was he heading our direction?

I'd never met the louse, but he could easily know what I looked like, and maybe Velda had told him about me…

Two tables over, he stopped and leaned in to speak to a middle-aged gent whose back was to me. Despite wearing what looked like an off-the-rack suit, the gent must have been money, because he had a platinum blonde baby doll at his table who was not likely his niece.

The middle-aged gent gestured for Quinn to sit down, and he did. Then the two were bending in close in confidential conversation, the older man turning his head sideways to do so.

That's when I realized who Quinn's friend was.

Mandel Meyers.

Mandy Meyers, the Jewish gangster who sat high up in a powerful Italian mob family in New York. Mandy Meyers, the strategic financial mastermind whose knowledge and skill in operating illegal gambling was second to none. Mandy Meyers, a modest-looking little man who could have you killed with a glance.

Quinn's silent partner in the casino here, maybe?

"Erin," I said, "would you excuse me? I just recognized a friend, and I really should say hello."

"Oh, that's fine."

"I might be a while. Order yourself another cocktail if you like."

"Listen, Mike, we can part company here. We're not on a date or anything. We're just a couple of people doing each other a favor."

"No, honey, stick around." I grinned. "Who knows? We're friends now. And friendship can lead to lots of things."

She smiled warmly at that, then blew me a little kiss as I headed across the room.

But if you think I was on my way to pay my respects to Mandy Meyers, you're wrong. And I wasn't interested in chatting with Nolly Quinn just yet, either...

When I sat down next to Velda, she jumped a little. Coming from a cool customer like her, that was equivalent to a nervous breakdown.

"Mike," she said. Her eyes were wide. "What are you doing here?"

"You first."

The sight of her, the smell of her, was making me drunker and crazier than anything a bartender could have served me up. My fists were taut and I could feel the things in my neck tighten and stand out.

"You need to leave," she said.

"I just got here, kitten."

"This isn't about you, Mike. You need to go."

I leaned closer. "Is it about Wade Manley? You do *know* he's dead, don't you?"

She swallowed. "I know he's dead. It's not about him. It's not about anything, Mike. I've just gone another way. What we had was swell, but it's over. You need to leave. You need to move on."

I rolled out the nasty grin that she knew so well. "Did you rehearse that, baby? Sorry it took me a while to get here. I took a detour into the drunk tank for a few months. But Pat hepped me about your location and status. Interesting. Wasn't I dangerous enough for you, kitten? Did you need a killer with no morals at all to satisfy your needs? You should have let me know. I would have tried harder."

She gripped my hand and squeezed it hard. Hard enough to hurt. "You need to go, Mike. You have *got* to go."

"Mike Hammer!"

I hadn't heard him coming up behind me, not over the latest rhumba. I turned and there he was, looming over me like a wax museum Cary Grant that the sculptor got just a little wrong. The cigarette holder was between two fingers at a jaunty angle. Like the way he held his head. Teeth gleaming white under the black strip of mustache. Eyes as dark and dead as a shark's.

His upper lip curled in something approaching a smile. "Welcome to Nolly Q's, Mr. Hammer."

He held a hand out for me to shake and I ignored it.

"Quite a place, Mr. Quinn. I don't remember a beer ever costing me a buck before."

He chuckled and reeled his hand back in, then resumed his seat next to Velda, putting her between us. He gestured with the cigarette holder, making figure-eight smoke trails. "Your money is no good here, Mr. Hammer. I'll make sure you're comped all down the line. Any friend of Velda's, after all."

"Oh," I said pleasantly, thinking about strangling him, "she's *mentioned* me."

"Yes, Mr. Hammer. Not frequently, I admit. But yes. She has. She said it was interesting working for you. I imagine it was. Notorious figure that you are."

"I guess I don't think of myself that way."

The sneer-smile resumed. "And I don't feel that way about myself, either, yet that's how the gutter press characterizes me. People can't know what it's like to live inside somebody else's skin, after all."

There was an idea: skin the bastard alive. That was one I'd never tried. Yet.

"Well," I said, "Miss Sterling may not have mentioned it, but I gave her that ring she's wearing."

"Oh, that cute little sapphire? Precious little thing. No, I did get the impression that you two had been… close. But all of us have our disappointments in love, Mr. Hammer. Or may I call you Mike?"

"Sure. Why not."

He lifted his chin as if to give me a better look at its cleft. "I understand you're an impulsive individual, Mike. I have a bad habit of giving in to emotionalism myself. But it's best for all concerned, when a love affair has run its course, to just… move on. I'm going to ask you to do that, Mike. Oh, I'm not asking you to leave town on the noon stage or any such nonsense. No. Enjoy yourself for a few days. Take a week. Take two. A lot to do in Miami Beach. Knock yourself out." The lilt left his voice. "But then go, Mike. Go, man. *Go.*"

"When Velda tells me to," I said.

"Listen to him, Mike," she said, turning to me with urgency, a wildness in her eyes.

"I catch the words, baby," I said. "But I don't hear the music."

Quinn rested his cigarette-in-holder in an ashtray. He folded his hands, which were heavy with diamonds riding heavy gold rings that really did put that sapphire to shame, and he said, "I am treating you with patience and respect, Mike. Out of courtesy to Miss Sterling. But if you do anything else that intrudes upon us—"

"Is that what I'm doing, Slick?"

He sighed in strained patience. "I'm not referring to you dropping by this club, which is after all a public place. I refer instead to you dropping by Miss Sterling's apartment today—one of my boys is in the hospital with a concussion, and the other one is laid up at home in bed, I'll have you know. If you—"

"*Nolly!*" The voice came from behind me, this time a feminine one: "Nolly? Can we please talk? In private?"

I glanced back and she was standing there, the beautiful waif in the green gown and all that crazy red hair. The lovely green eyes were shimmering with tears, her mascara trailing down her face, turning her tears black.

"Erin," Quinn said firmly, "you need to leave."

She came quickly around the table and hovered over him like a Christmas angel hanging on a string. "Don't let her move in with you, Nolly. She's not what you need. *I'm* what you need. You know I'm right."

His voice was flat. Merciless. "Erin. You're embarrassing yourself. Leave."

"Nolly, darling, please," she said, and she put her arm around him.

He rose, pushing her away. She was trying to keep her balance when he slapped her and she fell, knocking her into the next table, startling two couples who scooted back in alarm.

I was there before he even saw me move and I pasted him one in the mouth and bloodied up his handsome face. When he just stood there like a puppet whose strings went loose, I smacked him again, on the chin, and he went down like kindling.

I was on top of him, choking him, his face red and his eyes bulging, when two bouncers in tuxes pulled me off and dragged me out, my knees bumping down the short flight of steps before they dropped me on the sidewalk.

The only reason they didn't go to work on me right then was that several well-dressed couples were standing nearby frowningly reevaluating their choice of nightspots. When Nolly appeared at the top of the steps, the bouncers held me up by either arm and he waved his finger like a scolding parent.

"Next time you die, Hammer," he said through a bloody smear of a mouth.

"Somebody will," I said.

The customers scurried away and the bouncers hauled me around the side of the building, as if taking me to my car, but then worked me over instead.

I've taken worse beatings, but this was a thorough

professional job of it, anyway. Several fists to the face but no broken nose or teeth, enough punches to the breadbasket to drop me to my knees, and finally a few kicks in the ribs just to make sure I knew they weren't kidding. Somebody stuffed my hat on me and they dropped me in a pile and it was over before I'd even got a decent look at them. How the hell could a guy get even that way?

Then she was at my side, little Erin, her face a runny mess but her hair perfect, the angel hovering over me protectively. She helped me up and walked me the rest of the way to the parking lot. I managed to point her to my car and she helped me get in and behind the wheel.

We sat in the darkness a while regaining our breath and our dignity.

"Your place or mine?" I asked, only half-joking.

She only heard the other half, shaking her head, all that red hair moving like a choppy sea. "No... I can't... bad time."

"Yeah. Me, too."

The impish grin came back. "No. I mean... of the month." She reached a hand over and it settled in my lap. "There are other ways, Mike. Would serve them both right, them in there, us right behind them."

Her hand was moving expertly but nothing was happening. Sometimes a guy is just not in the mood.

I sent her hand back to her gently. Smiled at her. "Rain check, baby?"

"Rain check," she said, smiling, nodding, and slipped out of the car into the night.

CHAPTER SIX

The nightstand phone woke me. I fumbled for the thing, blinking at bright sun coming in through sheer curtains. With my other hand I grabbed my watch—half-past one. Hell! I'd slept twelve hours again.

"Good mornin', Mr. Hammer," Duffy's wife Martha whispered in my ear. She had a southern lilt that was more Carolina than Florida. "Or good afternoon, I guess I should say. Would you care to take a call from New York City?"

"Yeah," I said. "Thanks."

This was no surprise. Last night, before I hit the rack, I'd left word at Centre Street for Pat to call when he got in today.

I sat up, groaning some. It wasn't that the after-bender glow had worn off, like Duff predicted. The way I felt had nothing to do with booze. This was the aftermath of that expert beating I'd taken last night at Nolly Q's. None of my ribs seemed broken but I had purple blossoms on both sides, and polka dots of blue and yellow and purple on my chest and stomach. My upper torso looked like a sport shirt in terrible taste.

Martha put me through, and I said, "Hello, Pat?"

"Yeah. Sorry not to get back to you sooner, Mike."

It was a good connection. I stuffed a pillow between me and the headboard. "That's okay, pal. I slept in."

"Out on the town, huh? The Miami nightlife must suit you. Getting enough to drink, old buddy?"

"I'm sober as a parish priest, pal."

"So you say, but have you been hitting the sacramental wine?"

That made me laugh, which hurt a little. "Shit, man, I haven't had anything stronger than a brew since you saw me last."

A pause. Then: "You don't sound like it. You're breathing hard. You're like a dirty phone call."

"Yesterday I was floating on air. All the garbage was drained out of me and the world welcomed me back. Then I took a beating last night."

"How bad?" Was that actual concern in his voice?

"They were good. Real pros. Nothing shows on my face, no teeth missing, nothing broken, but I feel like a thumb that got caught in a car door."

"That's what they make aspirin for. So. If you're sober and a new man and all, how did you wind up rating a shellacking?"

"I'm still Mike Hammer, buddy. I was always able to get in jams drunk or sober."

I filled him in about the doings last night at Nolly Q's, including my brief conversation with Velda.

"Mike," he said, and the friend was back in his voice, "maybe she was playing it straight with you. Maybe she's just... moved on. It happens."

"No. She's up to something. I swear she's in Vice Squad mode. I think Wade Manley recruited her for an undercover assignment."

"Or maybe you just *want* to think that. Mike, Wade Manley's dead as hell and she's still down there. Who's she working for, if the boss already had his funeral?"

I put a shrug in my voice. "Herself maybe. I don't know. I have to get her alone and away from Quinn and his cronies, to really find out. She wasn't free to talk last night. Maybe she's got a program lined up and I don't fit in. But I'm going to."

"Mike. Are you sure you're not kidding yourself? We both know the lady has a thing for bad boys. A lot of dames do. And this Quinn character is even badder than you, buddy."

"No. He just thinks he is."

But Pat rattled on: "Nolly Quinn was a Murder Incorporated killer in his damn teens. When we were sweating it out in the jungle, he was running the top call girl operation in the city. And if anybody crosses him, he takes care of it personal."

"You know this for a fact, do you? Then why didn't

you boys in Homicide ever arrest his ass and slam it in Old Sparky? It's just talk, Pat. I had a steak yesterday tougher than that twerp. He slaps little girls around. He smokes with a cigarette holder, for Christ's sake."

"Don't underestimate him, pal. Hitler painted watercolors."

I was shaking my head at the phone, as if he could see me through it. "Pat, I don't underestimate Nolly Quinn's ability to be an evil prick. And while we both know Velda can take care of herself, I'm not sure she realizes what kind of danger she's in."

His tone went hushed. "You *really* think she's in danger?"

"Nolly Quinn runs through fluffs faster than Errol Flynn—only in Nolly's case, some of 'em wind up dead."

I told him how two of the gangster's recent girl friends had wound up a suicide and hit-and-run respectively.

His voice took on a somber note. "Mike, you get close to Velda fast. Get her the hell away from this bastard."

"You talked me into it. What have you come up with on your end? Anything?"

He let out something that was half-laugh, half-sigh. "I'll tell you one thing—the Big Man sure picked a lousy part of town to die in. Trying to canvass that area is like dropping the soap in a jailhouse shower— slippery and you can get nasty surprises."

"Nothing then?"

"I didn't say that. There must be a dozen rathole taverns down there, and I wanted to handle the interviews myself. So it took a while to turn anything. But in a charming joint called Dirty Dick's, a bartender finally made Manley's picture."

"Not as a regular customer surely?"

"Hell no. One time only, and while the apron couldn't be sure about the date, the timing seemed about right. Either around or on the night of his death, Wade Manley was seen talking to somebody in a back booth at Dirty Dick's."

"Talking to who, Pat?"

"Bartender didn't get a look at the guy."

"Was there a barmaid who might have?"

"Dirty Dick's doesn't have that rarefied level of service. You go up to the bar and cart your drinks back to wherever you're sitting. Our only shot is working our way through the colorful group that represents Dirty Dick's regular clientele. That fun job I turned over to two of my best men, who may never speak to me again."

Finally, a sliver of light…

I said, "If you can get a decent description, and maybe even a police artist's rendering, we may have a suspect."

"That's the idea. Mike, you and I should probably stay in touch. Daily calls. So, uh… really no cravings?"

"Yeah. And I quit smoking, too."

"The hell you say."

"I do say."

"And you aren't clawing the walls for a Lucky?"

"No. It helps when you get the shit beat out of you.

A hell of a useful distraction."

He laughed. It was good to hear. The ease of this conversation was a relief. I had plenty of friends and more friendly acquaintances than a happy hound dog. But there was only one guy worthy of the "best friend" designation, and that was Pat. His only rival for that title was a woman who was more than a best friend. Or maybe not a friend now at all, if I took her words at face value.

"Listen, Mike," he said, a shift in his tone, "what you told me about Quinn stopping at Mandy Meyers' table at that club last night? Could be significant."

"Shitbirds of a feather stink up the joint together, is what I take from it. Mandy's probably backing the casino play at Nolly Q's."

"Probably, but it could be more. You probably know Mandy Meyers is the reputed architect of the transfer of open gambling from Miami to Cuba. And Cuba is useful in other ways to guys like Meyers and the mob he represents."

"You mean like setting up a narcotics trafficking network," I said. "City editor at the *Herald* says word's already out that Quinn is involved in dope smuggling. Partners with Meyers? Rivals?"

"Did the conversation look tense?"

"No, but it seemed serious. Business, not social."

Another sigh. "Well, Mike, the word's out up here about something, too. It seems one of the five Mafia families… not sure which one yet… is jockeying to create a drug conduit from Cuba to Miami. Could be Mandy's the point man."

"And Quinn could be his boy, or his partner, or his competition."

"*Something* anyway," Pat said. "Worth keeping in mind. This is big, Mike. Big like in ramifications. Big like in repercussions."

Big like something Velda might go undercover to get?

"I'll keep it in mind, buddy," I said. "I'll check in with you tomorrow."

"Do that. If we get a break on the Big Man's murder, I'll call you."

We hung up.

Mid-afternoon, the city room at the *Herald* was hopping. Ben Sauer's office door stood half open and I stuck my head in. He was at his messy desk, attending to curling sheets of copy. The only thing that had changed since the other night was the hulking city editor had traded in his red suspenders for blue.

"Lousy timing, I know," I said.

But the horsey face only smiled and waved me in and to shut the door, then gestured to the hardwood chair opposite him.

"Glad for the break," he said. "A relief to talk to somebody who isn't ink-stained and keyed-up."

I sat.

A grin formed under the battered nose. "Sticking to

that four-beer-a-day regimen, Mike?"

"Only had three yesterday."

"Good for you, man." Then he reached down and got his bottle out of that lower desk drawer. Testing me, maybe. Or just thirsty. He was the kind of guy who was thirsty all day long. And night.

Pouring himself half a water glass of brown nectar, he said, "I've been hoping you'd stop by. You should have left me your phone number."

I folded my arms. "I'm at the Sea Breeze Motel. I don't know the number, but I bet you have the staff to ferret that out."

He chuckled at that and had a sip of whiskey, leaving the bottle on his desk. "There's a guy I know who'd like to talk to you."

"Is it somebody I'd *want* talking to me?"

"Maybe. First things first, though. What brings you around to my hidey hole, Mike? Getting anywhere on your inquiry? Or is it a quest?"

I figured that was rhetorical, and skipped straight to a condensed recap of what happened last night.

He rocked back in his chair, a wide smile splitting the well-grooved face. "So you pasted Nolly in his own joint, huh? And lived to tell the tale! More than most could say."

"I don't know." I shrugged. "I figure he hardly ever kills anybody right there in the club."

The editor let out a small laugh. "You may have something there." He gave me an appraising look.

"How bad did his boys work you over?"

"Thorough but restrained. I'm walking around, aren't I?"

"Well, not to be literal, but right now you're sitting down." He sipped whiskey. "What can I do for Mike Hammer?"

"I could use a rundown on Quinn's daily schedule, for one thing."

He got thoughtful, raised a finger, and pushed a button on his phone to get an outside line. I frowned and he shook the finger at me, then used it to dial a number.

Half a dozen rings later, somebody answered. A male voice, I thought, but that's all I could make out.

Sauer said, "That party you said you'd like to meet is sitting in my office."

I frowned again and was half-way out of my chair when the editor raised a stop hand, and nodded for me to sit back down.

"…I think he'll meet with you, yes. If you can do him a small favor… Well, he needs a rundown on Nolly Quinn's activities, and who better…? A daily schedule kind of thing… Yes. Yes, I'll tell him."

He hung up.

I studied him but the well-worn face wasn't giving me anything. He was jotting something down on a notepad. Then he tore off a slip and handed it over to me, like I was his patient and this was the prescription.

He said, "If you want that information, Mike, here's where you should be in one hour. I wouldn't be late. This is a punctual person."

"Who *is* this 'person?'"

"You'll find out when you get there."

"*If* I go there."

He spread his hands. The right was ink-stained. "If you want the rundown on Quinn you requested, that's where you'll be in an hour. Up to you. I'm just passing it along."

I showed him my teeth. It was only a smile by definition. "Like you passed along what you knew about me to this 'punctual person?'"

He finished his whiskey, rocking back gently, smiling at me like a plantation owner on a porch in the glow of a mint julep.

"I'm a newspaperman, Mike. You're a private detective. We have something in common. We deal in information. Often we acquire more information by trading other information. That's how it works for both of us, in both our fields, right?"

"Mostly I just beat it out of people."

He smiled, started to chuckle but it got caught in his throat. His eyebrows went up. "Trust me on this, Mike. You do want to meet this individual, but it's not my place to say more at the moment. And if it turns out you don't, uh, hit it off? Well, then, you just walk away… Is there anything else I can help you with?"

"I don't know, Ben. I don't have anything else to trade. I already emptied the bag about last night at Nolly Q's."

He patted the air like a lazy crossing guard. "Oh, that filled your account up nicely. Go ahead. What else can I tell you?"

I sucked in air and let some out. "Ben, this is something you might not know off the top of your head. You might have to do a little digging."

"Try me."

"You're aware that two of Quinn's former flames got snuffed, right? At least that's how I figure it."

He frowned in thought with some curiosity mixed in, then leaned forward. "Dorothy Flynn, hatcheck girl at his club. A suicide. Kimberly Carter, the singer. Hit-and-run victim. Closed cases, Mike. Not murders. Not officially."

"What do *you* think, Ben? Unofficially?"

His shrug was expansive. "I don't know what to think. He's a ladies' man. He breaks hearts left and right. I could buy some sensitive kid who got the boot doing the Dutch act. Having another recent ex get run down by a drunk driver… is that a tragic coincidence? Or does it strain credulity?"

"It strains something."

He gestured to the file cabinets behind him. "Mike, you want to see the files on the two dead girls? They're part of what I've salted away on Quinn."

"Not right now. I'm not interested in dead girls. You can't talk to dead girls."

"Not without a Ouija board. What do you have in mind?"

"I want the names of any other dames this road company Romeo's thrown over in the past year and a half. I want their whereabouts, their addresses. According to Barney Pell, at least a couple of them are still in Greater Miami."

He was rocking again, but it was steady and shallow now. "You're talking to Pell, huh? And here I figured maybe you were tryin' to fly under the police radar."

I gave him a real grin this time. "No, I like to keep the cops informed… up to a point. Nice to have them handy. And they're always kind of naturally a couple steps behind me."

He was smiling. Nodding. He jotted some notes down. "I'll get back to you on that. At the Sea Breeze?"

"At the Sea Breeze." I got up. "Thanks."

"Off so soon?"

"Yeah. There's somebody I have to meet. Remember?"

He was pouring himself another half a glass as I went out.

Miami Beach was a long, narrow island connected to the mainland by four causeway bridges and a shorter one at the northern tip. Somehow in that limited space, hundreds of gleaming white hotels and motels managed to pack themselves in along the oceanfront.

I was strolling the grounds of one of the biggest hotels on Collins Avenue. Between it and the beach was a terraced area with colorful cabanas, royal palms, an outdoor bar, and a cluster of white wrought-iron tables, the whole mess centered around a huge amoeba-shaped pool where a handful of young and beautiful guests swam and splashed. The kiddie pool was conspicuously empty, as if these thoroughbreds hadn't gotten around to making babies just yet. Another sprinkling of what I took to be honeymooners were sunning poolside on lounge-style deck chairs, boy-girl-boy-girl. Sitting here and there at tables under umbrellas, taking in the moving tapestry of youthful flesh, were senior-citizen guests in clothes so gaudy a golfer would heave. Off-season here seemed divided between the newly married and heaven's waiting room.

The bored-looking Cuban bartender in the short-sleeve shirt and bow tie seemed disappointed when all I wanted was a beer. He served it up in a pilsner and with my rump half on a stool and my back to the bar, I surveyed the area. It took three whole seconds to spot him.

Feds are always easy to make. They have hair longer than G.I.s and shorter than civilians. They wear suits that aren't flashy but always look new and pressed, dark but not black, with white shirts. Their ties are always a little narrower than the fashion, unless the fashion is narrow, when they go a little wider. Their hats have a front pinched-crown and snapped brim and no feather. Their shoes are Florsheims with a military shine. They are not just clean-shaven, but twice-a-day shaven. They have faces so blank it's like they've never been used. When they smile you can only see it if you're really paying attention. They don't drink on the job. They make carrying a gun seem dull.

But my fed was trying to fit in. Substitute above where applicable: a cream-color linen suit; green-and-yellow pastel striped tie; white straw fedora with black band; and white bucks. Add black sunglasses, and a glass of iced tea with lemon. Top it off with a huge red-and-blue umbrella shielding the white table where he sat alone, facing the swimming pool.

I sat next to him and put my beer on the table. "Red-and-blue umbrella to one side of the bar, like the instructions said. Next time try sunbathing on Old Glory—you'll be easier to spot."

Who was I to talk? In my suit and tie I was about as touristy as a vacuum cleaner salesman.

He turned toward me barely and one of those smiles you had to know how to catch formed on a well-tanned anonymous face that was largely obscured by the sunglasses. What still showed was the kind of blandly handsome features you see in Sears catalogues.

He extended a hand below the edge of the metal table as if he were passing me microfilm. His handshake was as firm as it was perfunctory. "Michael Hammer. Thank you for seeing me."

"Do you have a name or a number or anything? What, FBI? No… FBN, right? This would be a federal narcotics investigation. After all, Hoover's gang thinks the Mafia is a myth. Like the Loch Ness monster and a free lunch."

His voice was soft with an edge. "You're as big a character as I've heard, Mr. Hammer."

A bouncy blonde in a bikini was pretending she wanted to get away from the young guy pursuing her. I was glad no lifeguard was around to tell her no running around the pool.

I asked, "Why would the FBN have heard of me?"

He sipped his iced tea. "Two years ago, you were implicated in the deaths of several key figures in a major Mafia narcotics ring." The barely imperceptible smile returned briefly. "Yes, Mr. Hammer, the FBN *does* believe in the Mafia."

I watched the blonde caper some more. "I was questioned about that. Never went anywhere."

"I said 'implicated.' And our friends at the CIA consider you the probable key figure in a major if hushed-up incident involving the deaths of some seventy-eight agents of Communist Russia, including the only Soviet operatives ever discovered on American soil."

A very cute brunette in a two-piece bathing suit was sitting on the edge of the pool next to a young guy who was probably her brand-new husband. I hoped he knew what a lucky bastard he was.

"That I wasn't even questioned about," I said. "Anyway, seventy-eight strikes me as a little low. Do you or don't you have a name, buddy? A phony one will do."

His lips pursed in mild irritation. "My name is Jones, and it's not phony. Do you need to see credentials?"

"Naw. But if you're not a fed, you should hire out to kids' parties as one." The brunette and her guy were kissing in front of God and everybody. "Mr. Jones, you know what I want from you—Nolly Quinn's daily routine."

"Let's not get ahead of ourselves, Mr. Hammer."

I sipped the beer. It felt nice not to gulp it. Nicer that it just seemed refreshing and not like life's blood anymore.

I said, "If this is where you tell me to butt out, because I'm interfering with a government operation and would spoil months of work and yackata yackata, then save yourself the trouble."

He shook his head and that damn faint smile returned. It even hung around. "Nothing like that, Mr. Hammer. Don't quote me, but I'm pleased... *others* are pleased, as well... that you've taken a personal interest in Nolly Quinn."

I stopped looking at broads in bikinis and turned to stare into the agent's sunglasses. The rest of his face had no more expression than they did. "Now you've really lost me, Jonesy."

He flipped a hand. "Mr. Quinn has indeed been the focus of an FBN operation... but it's one that was recently suspended due to insufficient cause."

"What does that mean?"

Something human came into his voice. "It means that a team of three working six months couldn't get a damn thing on somebody as slippery and well-insulated as Nolly Quinn. He makes occasional trips to Cuba, and several associates of his do the same, rather more frequently. He communicates with any number of freelance fliers, as well as the captains of various vessels, both commercial and recreational. In no instance have we ever seen an exchange of money, nor any transfer of contraband."

"What about on the Cuban end?"

Displeasure registered however faintly. "We're not authorized to operate outside of the USA."

I grinned at this idiocy. "Well, your 'friends' in the CIA sure as hell can and do, don't they?"

He paused, probably as he decided how much he dared parcel out to me. "For reasons we can't discern, there is little or no interest from those quarters in helping us on that front. It's possible… and I say this very much off the record, Mr. Hammer… that Nolly Quinn is an asset of theirs."

"Quinn in bed with the CIA? You have got to be shitting me."

He indulged himself in a tiny sigh. "Would that it were so, Mr. Hammer. But it's a big, dirty, complicated world out there, and strange bedfellows seem to be requisite in international espionage."

"So your operation has been shut down?"

He nodded. "I'm the only agent left. My office is in Miami." He took a card from his suit coat's breast pocket and handed it over. "I've written a private number there as well, should you require my support."

I eyeballed the card. "Really? John Jones?"

The faint smile again. "Somebody has to be. Otherwise it wouldn't be so common, would it?"

I shifted in the wrought-iron chair. "Reading between the lines, Jonesy, I figure you might like having me around causing trouble for Quinn. Might make up for what you couldn't pull off."

"Something like that." Another tiny sigh. "But as for your request, I'm afraid I can't help you out on Quinn's daily routine."

"Don't tell me *that's* top secret."

"No, Mr. Hammer. Nolly Quinn doesn't *have* a daily routine. He has half a dozen legitimate business interests, from fruit to construction. And there's his nightclub, where he sometimes is on hand for four or five nights out of a week, and other times skips a week entirely. He spends an unspecified amount of time tending to his various business interests. In no particular order. At no particular time of day."

I frowned. "That nightclub—if Uncle Whiskers wants Nolly Quinn taken down so bad, why doesn't the FBI bust his ass over that wide-open casino he runs?"

Then a little sound emerged that must have been a laugh. "Are you familiar with the system of law enforcement in Miami-Dade County?"

"Sort of. Just a little more corrupt than Chicago and ten times as complicated, right?"

He nodded. "Twenty-six independent incorporated

communities, including Miami and Miami Beach, each with its own police force, plus winding in and around those is unincorporated territory handled by the sheriff's metro division. It's a recipe for chaos, and for corruption."

I was shaking my head. "But after that Senate fuss, the FBI shut down the gambling in this town."

"Most of it. There are exceptions, Mr. Hammer, and Nolly Q's is a major one. That casino is protected, and before any federal raid is made, Quinn is warned and a procedure goes into effect that turns that gambling den into a big empty storeroom in under an hour."

"Sounds like somebody ought to just kill the bastard."

Agent Jones said nothing, sipping his iced tea.

I sat forward and stared right into those sunglasses. "Jones, have you people sent an agent in, to infiltrate Quinn's set-up? A woman maybe?"

His mouth twitched. "If you mean your friend Miss Sterling, no. She's not one of ours."

I wasn't sure whether that was good news or bad. "Were you working in tandem with NYPD Vice? Specifically with Captain Wade Manley?"

"No." His tone turned somber. "I knew him, of course, and I understand you were his friend. He was a fine officer, and a good man. You have my sympathy for your loss."

I kept pressing. "Did you uncover anything that might have linked Quinn to Manley's murder, no matter how vague? How tenuous?"

He shook his head. "Nothing. And I only have one other piece of information for you, Mr. Hammer. Not, I'm afraid, anything that you will be pleased to hear."

"What?"

"Your friend Velda moved in with Quinn today."

CHAPTER SEVEN

After my meeting with Agent Jones, I was in the hotel's underground parking garage heading to the Ford when I noticed a little guy in his fifties strolling down the row of cars. He was walking a tiny dog, a Pomeranian, like maybe he thought cement would do just as well as grass for his little explosion of orange and white fur.

I was about to get in the convertible when I got the sense he was heading my way. Just another retiree type. Cream-color knit sport shirt, yellow slacks and sandals with socks, a dark tan that was a collaboration between God and Florida. Miami Beach was full of guys like this.

Then as he drew nearer I got a better look at the oval face with its smart monkey features—narrow close-set eyes, weak chin, slicked back dark hair going gray.

Mandy Meyers.

No bodyguards were in view, and he was clearly

unarmed, just the two of us in the empty cavern of cars. Three, counting the pooch. But just the same, my hand lifted itself as if unbidden to where the .45 in the shoulder sling lurked under my unbuttoned suit coat.

He paused and lifted his hand like an unlikely pope making a benediction. His Pomeranian took the opportunity to lift its leg, not in benediction. Meyers waited patiently for it to finish, neither man nor beast having any compunction about soiling a public place.

Then as if following the trail of dog piss down the slope of cement, he came over saying in a measured baritone, just loud enough to echo, "No need for that, Mr. Hammer."

He meant I didn't need to take my rod out and rid the world of him. I wasn't sure I agreed.

"Just out walking the dog, Mr. Meyers?" We'd never met but he knew me all right, and I felt I knew him. We occasionally made the same tabloids. "Always nice to get a little fresh air. Hard to beat an auto ramp for that."

"No need to drag out your wit, either, Mr. Hammer. I'm not here to duel, with words or… anything else. I just have an invitation for you. A request."

"Okay."

"A few close friends of mine are getting together for drinks in a suite at the Betsy Ross Hotel this afternoon. We'd like you to join us."

"When exactly is this cocktail party?"

The dog was looking at its master and then at me and back again. It had done its business, after all, and the tiny black eyes in the blast of orange fur were wondering why the hold-up.

The gangster's smile was small yet enormously unsettling. "Why, right *now*, Mr. Hammer."

"You want me to come with you, Meyers? I don't see any muscle making me."

The laugh that came out of that thin cut of a smile was equally small. Equally awful. "No one's going to force you into the back of a black limousine at gunpoint, Mr. Hammer. No one's taking you for a ride. I do my best not to deal in clichés."

The Pomeranian had gotten bored and tested the limit of its leash, then began leaving a little brown present near a Cadillac.

I said, "I guess I've been dealing with an uncouth breed of hoodlum up to now."

The smile disappeared and the slitted eyes grew hard. His monkey face suddenly had real jungle in it.

"There's no need for insults, Mr. Hammer. I try to make sure my approach with other professionals has a basis in mutual respect. This is just an invitation, like I said, a request… and you are free to decline. But I think it would be advantageous for you to accept. Possibly even lucrative."

I shook my head and grinned at him. "I'm not getting in a car with you, Meyers, whether you got muscle or guns or not. Leave it at not wanting that dog shedding on me. Give me the room number and maybe I'll meet you over there."

That seemed to satisfy him. "It's the Paul Revere Suite. On the third floor. Do you know the way to the Betsy? It's in South Beach."

"Stick a lamp or two in the window, and I'll see if I can track it down."

His upper lip twitched. "I'm sure you will, a detective of your skills."

He and the dog started off, and I called to them.

"By the way, Meyers, how is it we just happened to run into each other, here in this particular parking garage?"

His expression was as bland as his tone. "We didn't."

"Starting to sound like maybe you're the detective."

"No. It's just that we keep an eye on the feds around here, and who they talk to."

Then he gave me a nod and a little wave, and he and the mutt moved on.

Amid the curves and geometry of so many Miami Beach hotels, the three-story Betsy Ross was resolutely old-fashioned, from its four-column portico to its shuttered windows. Having only whiteness and palm trees in common with its streamlined neighbors, the Colonial-style hotel offered seclusion and privacy even at the height of busy season. In off-times like this, the Betsy was an elegant old Southern mansion suitable for haunting. With no ghosts available, gangsters would have to do.

With its churning ceiling fans, potted palms and

Early American furnishings, the lobby looked like a turn-of-the-century outpost in Guam. The small bar seemed to have been invaded by a convention of wrestlers, eight heavies sitting around small tables reading *The Racing News*, *Ring* and *Confidential* with bottles of Coke in front of them. Maybe it was a book club with a chat session later. First topic of discussion might be the bulges under their left arms.

I took a self-service elevator that didn't remind me at all of 1776. On three, I moved down a hallway with blue Liberty Bell-pattern carpeting, then knocked at a door with a gold plaque that read *Paul Revere Suite* in old-timey script.

Mandy Meyers himself, still in casual attire right down to his socks and sandals, answered the door and flashed that same nearly invisible smile.

He said, "Good," and gestured me into a living room that gave no hint that we were in the Orange State beyond sunlight streaming through filmy-curtained windows framed by ruffled valances. The walls were hung with gilt-framed Revolutionary War prints and portraits of Washington and Jefferson, and the colors ran to burnt reds and muted greens. Like the lobby, the furniture was Early American, too new-looking to be antiques.

The only genuine antiques in the room were Meyers and three other senior citizens. More like Early Twentieth Century than Early American. No sign of the Pomeranian, so maybe I wouldn't have to watch my step.

Or would I?

The other three gents were just as casually dressed as Meyers, but you would mistake them for harmless retirees at your own peril.

Seated on a cushioned maple couch were Alberto Bonetti, head of one of the five New York Mafia families, and next to him Carlo Civella, top dog of the Chicago Outfit. On a matching chair nearby perched Santo De Luca, Detroit mob boss who dated back to Purple Gang days.

Nobody got up upon my entrance, and nobody offered a hand to shake. I didn't offer my hand to anybody, either.

Meyers dragged an unpadded birch chair over for me to sit and face this distinguished group. Then he took a hard chair at Bonetti's end of the couch, and sat with arms folded and legs crossed. There was no sign of refreshments at this supposed cocktail party. It felt like I was applying for a job.

Bonetti took the lead. He was a big man with a well-grooved oval face and slicked-back salt-and-pepper hair, though his black eyebrows were stark black and thick as three-ply carpet. Big dockworker hands lay limp in his lap. He was an executive now, but had killed many men in his day.

"Mr. Hammer," he said, in an affable growl, "we appreciate you stopping by."

"Always up for a party."

"It's a real show of good faith, you accepting

Mandy's invite. A demonstration of respect, and that is also appreciated. In that same spirit, you'll note that no one has asked you to stand for a frisk. And that we four are alone, without our usual, you know, staff members on hand."

I smiled. "I saw your boys in the bar downstairs. You'll be glad to know nobody was drinking on the job. They've turned the place into a Christian Science Reading Room."

Bonetti smiled a little, perhaps just to be polite. The other three didn't. Tough room.

Civella picked up. He was a medium-sized guy with stark white hair in a Julius Caesar cut, and the same dark eyebrows as Bonetti. Cheekbones prominent, eyes hooded, he sported a funeral home pallor that Florida had done nothing about.

"We've never had dealings, Mr. Hammer," Civella said, his voice smoothly uninflected. "But we're aware of your skills and of course your reputation. We would like to discuss hiring you."

"I make a point of not hiring out to people in your line of business."

Now De Luca, skinny, fox-faced, chimed in. "We ain't approaching you in *that* business capacity, Mr. Hammer. We don't do that type of business in Miami. Which is the goddamn *point*."

If it was, I didn't get it.

Bonetti stayed low-key. "That's not to say we don't do business in Miami. After the feds came down hard on gambling here, we moved out into legit endeavors. Plenty of ways to make an honest dollar around here—construction, nightclubs, hotels, jukeboxes, liquor distribution, waste disposal. All very profitable and honest enterprises, Mr. Hammer."

Civella sat forward and gestured with an open hand. "In addition to our legitimate business interests, Mr. Hammer, individually and together, we each of us has a winter home down here. Often bring our wives, and frequently our grown kids and grandkids come to visit. It's an old tradition going back to Al and Frank."

Capone and Nitti. Well-known family men.

De Luca, who was edgier than the others, was damn near falling off his chair. "We are not going to have no prick upstart put all of that at *risk*! We got good goddamn will goin' down here. We're solid citizens!"

"I believe you," I said. "And I might know what prick upstart you mean."

Meyers finally joined in.

"I'm at fault here," he began, and the others waved that off, saying, "No, no, oh no!" and so on.

But he continued: "I'm the one took Nolly Quinn under his wing. I knew him for over ten years, way back when he was a fresh-faced kid taking on his first contracts. I watched him put together the top call girl ring in Manhattan! Enough to make a guy proud. Then he wanted to retire down here, at age thirty-five no less, and do some dabbling in business, he said. And now he's in construction with Alberto over there, and fruit and vegetables with Carlo."

De Luca piped up, "I don't do *nothin'* with him!"

Meyers plowed on. "I went in with Nolly in that nightclub of his. I negotiated with local officials to put in a casino, with assurances that we would not expand past that point. It's been going over a year and so far so good."

Bonetti raised one black eyebrow. "But now this punk kid is gettin' big ideas. He's running *dope* through here from Cuba, though he swears up and down he ain't. Now, you might think that Miami would make us a natural contraband conduit, and who knows? Maybe someday it will—"

"Never!" Meyers snapped.

Raising a hand, Bonetti said, "That's a discussion for another day… but for now, and we all of us in this room agree, narcotics are strictly off-limits in Miami. Just too goddamn risky. Hell, it's less than two years since that federal gambling crackdown. We are in the meantime minting money in our legit enterprises. Plus, as far as that particular type of merchandise is concerned, we already have sufficient European supply routes. And, like Carlo said, we winter with our goddamn *families* here! We *live* here half the damn time. And where I come from—which is where *you* come from, Mr. Hammer—a person does not shit where he eats."

Hanging his head, Meyers said, "I'm afraid I gotta plead mea culpa again."

This time nobody disagreed with him.

He was saying, "I viewed that boy like the son I never had, and now he's like the son I wish I'd *never* had." He sighed heavily. "But when I was moving my gambling interests to Cuba, I took Nolly along the first few times. He's very presentable, that boy. And apparently he made connections behind my back."

Disgusted, De Luca said something in Sicilian.

Bonetti said, his voice as reasonable and calm as a marriage counselor's, "Mr. Hammer, we believe in this instance we got a mutual interest with you. We are aware that you came to town on account of Nolly being shacked up with that secretary of yours. She is a lovely girl and also good with a .32, I hear. Anyway, we can certainly see why you would have a grievance with Nolly Quinn. A score to settle."

I saw an opening and took it. "What do you know about the murder of Wade Manley, Mr. Bonetti? How about you, Mr. Meyers? That was in your town, right? The one you fellas don't shit in?"

Meyers held up a hand like he was getting sworn in. "I had my problems with Manley going back to Luciano days. I don't deny it. But I respected the Big Man. And anyway, cops are off limits. Remember what happened to Dutch Schultz? I think I can speak for all of us in that regard."

Nodding, Bonetti said, "Mandy speaks for me, all right. I never put the finger on a cop in my life. But I *will* say this, Mr. Hammer… I am personally convinced that Nolly Quinn had a hand in the Manley kill."

Frowning skeptically, Meyers said, "He was in Florida at the time."

Bonetti shook his head. "Don't matter. He a hundred percent had it done. I heard it on good authority that somebody doing business with Quinn did that crime."

I said, "Seems to me there are several people in this *room* who're in business with Nolly Quinn."

"*Not me!*" De Luca exploded.

Civella said, "With the exception of Mandy's piece of that casino, all of our enterprises involving Quinn are on the up and up."

All very interesting if not terribly surprising.

I said, "So where do I come in?"

"You, Mr. Hammer," Bonetti said, the big hands on his knees now, "come in where we can't. Our standing as respectable businessmen and good winter citizens of Greater Miami would be called into question if there were a, uh… how shall I put it?"

"Gangland-style slaying," I said.

He nodded. "Yes. That's how the papers would label it. And we can't have that. So we would like to, well—*encourage* you in your efforts."

I frowned. "Encourage my efforts?"

He nodded toward Meyers. "Mandy saw you confront Quinn at his club."

"What I did," I said, "was belt him one and I had him about half-way strangled when his goon squad dragged me off."

"Those were probably bouncers," Bonetti said with a smile. He glanced at Meyers, who confirmed that with a nod. "You'd no doubt like to get him away from his protectors. That nightclub of his is the worst place to do that. Bouncers all over that joint. But his regular crew is limited to a couple of washed-up fighters."

I said, "A blond bozo and a knuckle-dragger? We've met."

"They're more flunkies than bodyguards," Bonetti said with offhand contempt. "Nolly is a cocky son of a bitch, with plenty of self-confidence. Good and goddamn casual about goin' around by himself, nobody to back him up. If you want to corner Nolly Quinn, Mr. Hammer, it shouldn't be that damn difficult."

I shook my head. "Tracking him seems to be. He doesn't follow any regular schedule."

Bonetti nodded. "True. But we might be able to help on that score." He glanced around and got some nods. He dug in his pocket and handed me a slip of paper. "You can reach me there. If I don't know where Nolly is, any given day, and what he's up to, one of my friends here likely will."

Civella said, "He has a meeting with me in an hour in Miami at our produce warehouse. Should last the rest of the afternoon."

Bonetti locked eyes with me and said, "If there's any other information you need, Mr. Hammer, just ask. Call any time. For instance, Quinn owns two cars. A black '54 Cadillac convertible and a white '52 Jaguar convertible."

"You've lost me," I said. "Where do I come in again?"

De Luca snarled, *"We want you to* kill *the bastard!"*

I guess I'd seen it coming, but hearing it like that still had some shock value, and I couldn't help but grin.

Bonetti leaned forward again, smiling like your favorite uncle, the fingers of his big hands interlaced and hanging between his spread knees. "We're inclined to think you'll likely do that, anyway, Mr. Hammer. But we've asked you here today to offer you... an incentive."

I hadn't seen the briefcase tucked alongside the couch next to where Civella sat. He reached down and brought it up and over the couch arm to set it in his lap like a salesman's sample case. He unsnapped it and swiveled it around to show me the contents.

Rows and rows of stacked green. Image after image of Benjamin Franklin, to join in with his fellow founding fathers around us.

"One hundred thousand dollars, Mr. Hammer," Bonetti said. "No fussing around with so-much-down, so-much-later. This is payment in full. We have no doubt that you can get this job done. Like Carlo says, your reputation precedes you."

I frowned. I waved a finger at the open briefcase. "Close that thing up," I said.

Frowning in confusion, Civella shut the case.

"Not enough?" Bonetti asked.

"Plenty. Generous. But I don't want your money."

Bonetti's expression registered mild irritation. "If

your eccentric sense of morality forbids you indulging money from shady sources, Mr. Hammer, why don't you just consider these funds as coming from the legitimate side of our enterprises? Why not view this as a retainer from some upstanding businessmen and citizens here in Miami?"

Who were hiring a murder.

"No," I said.

"No?" De Luca blurted. His face was radish red.

It occurred to me then what a favor I'd be doing the world to just pull my *Betsy out from under my arm and riddle these four evil bastards with .45 slugs.*

But tomorrow another four would just take their places, and today I'd have to blast my way out of here through the eight triggers downstairs.

And I had things to do before I died.

"You don't have to pay me, boys," I said, getting up. "This one's on the house."

The red-tile-roofed pink stucco one-and-a-half story just off Collins Avenue probably dated to the '20s when the Miami real estate boom went bust. But the Mediterranean Revival near-mansion had been refurbished in recent years and must be worth a pile now. A six-foot gated black wrought-iron fence in front and equally high hedges along the sides down to the oceanfront kept most people out.

I just pushed through.

This I did along one side of the place, via a less secluded yard next door. Any noise I made was covered by music coming from either a radio or a portable phonograph around back—Doris Day singing "Secret Love." The hedge left just enough room to allow me to move down a flagstone path that widened into a patio with a big kidney-shaped swimming pool. Its waters were gleaming like somebody had pitched in handful after handful of diamonds.

On a beach towel on the flagstone, a beautiful woman lay on her stomach, sunning in the nude, her face turned away from me, her dark hair damp from a recent swim. A white terry-cloth robe was slung over the back of a white wrought-iron chair nearby, at a matching table that was home to a red Bakelite portable radio. Doris kept singing. The beauty just kept sunning. I just kept looking.

She had a long lovely back, sloping gently to the narrow waist that curved back to her hips, the firm dimpled roundness of her bottom the gateway to long, sleek legs, a little heavier than Hollywood would have it. The tan was coming along nicely, a healthy golden glow.

"You're done on this side," I said.

Velda yelped a little and turned over fast, reaching for the robe. When she saw it was me, she still went for the robe but was in no hurry slipping it on, her expression running a gambit of emotions from relief to fear, from joy to dread. I stood there rocking on my gum-soled shoes, looking casual, as if glimpsing the full high breasts and flat muscular stomach and the tangle of dark hair at the V of her thighs didn't tear me apart like some rabid animal was ripping at my guts.

"Mike," she breathed, eyes flaring, nostrils too. The raven-wing hair made delicious gypsy tendrils. "You mustn't be here."

I pulled up one of the white wrought-iron chairs and sat down. "And yet I am."

She got up and took the chair where the robe had been draped, reaching to turn down the radio, where Tony Bennett had just begun "Rags to Riches." Her elbows were on the table and she was so close to me I could smell the suntan oil. No make-up. Just sheer classic beauty.

"You *have* to go," she said, the deep brown eyes begging me. "This is beyond dangerous."

"Then why don't you come with me?"

"How the hell did you get in here?"

"A little greenery isn't going to keep me away from my girl. You *are* still my girl, aren't you, kitten?" I touched her hand, the one with the sapphire ring, and she drew it away like a hot stove had touched her.

Her chin was up. "I told you last night, Mike. It's over between us. You need to move on. We had something wonderful, but—"

"Bullshit. And here I used to think you could have made it in the movies. I have my own ideas about what you're up to here, and why you don't think you can involve me. But I know you're still mine. It makes my skin crawl to think of you with that bastard, but…"

You could still hear the song playing, faintly, on the radio. I swept it off the table and it broke into pieces on the flagstone.

Velda jumped a little. But only a little.

"…but baby, I *know* you're still mine."

"No, Mike. *Go*. I told you before that—"

"I'll go. I'll leave you to your handsome keeper. And I'll stay out of it. I won't even chop the son of a bitch into pieces. Just tuck my tail between my legs and head back to Manhattan. But first, tell me this, doll. *Tell me why you held onto that picture of us, and hid it away.*"

Her eyes were jeweled with tears and she reached for my hand and held it and squeezed. She was swallowing and then about to speak when a male voice behind her intruded.

"*Well, Mr. Hammer!*" Nolly Quinn said.

A slender young dark-haired servant with a white jacket and a black mustache was holding open a sliding glass door and pointing to us.

Quinn came over, in no hurry. He looked like he'd walked out of a men's fashion spread in his off-white linen suit, cream-color shirt and chocolate tie. The young butler shut himself back inside the house.

"I'm rather relieved it's you," Quinn said, looming over us. "Half an hour ago, my houseboy noticed someone suspicious who was apparently casing the place, and gave me a call. I rushed right over."

He came around the table and took the remaining wrought-iron seat, putting himself between us. Elbows on the arms of the chair, he knitted his fingers at his chest. His expression, even his manner, seemed pleasant enough.

"Boy's too tightly wound," Quinn said regretfully, "and I really should give him the boot. But Ron does everything around here, cleaning, cooking. After all, lovers come and go, but a good servant is hard to find."

This seemed to be a not too subtle message to Velda, who said, "Mike stopped by unannounced, Nolly. I've just asked him to go. I've made it clear that—"

"She *has* made it clear," I said. "And I apologize for showing up here today. And even more for making a scene last night."

He touched his throat, smiling, raising an eyebrow. "Rather more than just a *scene*, I'd say… but believe me, I do understand. That girl I slapped… that was simply unacceptable. It's just that she's a crazy possessive little bitch, and… well, sometimes people just don't understand when a love affair is over."

"Some*times*," I said.

"Anyway, Mr. Hammer… Mike? Apology accepted." A smile blossomed under the Gable mustache. "*Apologies* accepted. But I don't think it serves any purpose for us to prolong this discussion… do you?"

"No," I said.

And it was the truth. It was all I could do not to pistol-whip him here and now.

But I wanted more. I wanted the goods on this bastard, and I needed to stop acting like a spurned, wronged lover and get back to some real detective work. Once I'd proved he was a murderer, it would be much easier to get away with killing him.

"I'll walk you out," he said, the perfect host. "I'll have to let you out the front gate."

Quinn took the lead and I gave Velda a backward glance that said, *Later, kitten.* I followed him down the flagstone path and around to the gate. There he used a little intercom to have the houseboy unlock it from inside. It opened automatically, swinging out a little and then all the way back in. The thing must have dated back as far as the house, because it creaked like a door in a haunted-house picture.

He said, "Mr. Hammer... Mike... I choose to believe you've been sincere with me today. Velda is a very special girl, and she and I are at the beginning of something that I think could last a very long while. You need to know that I fight for what I want, Mike, and that your well-earned reputation does not dissuade me in the least. *I* came up on the streets, too."

That had seemed friendly and reasonable and not at all the threat of death that it was.

Velda came rushing out of somewhere, still in the robe, her hair nearly dry from the afternoon sun. "Mike!"

We had both already turned to her when she approached us, took my right hand with both of hers. "Mike, I'm so sorry to have hurt you. And I want you to know how very grateful I am that you're taking this so well."

She flashed me a brave little smile, then took Nolly's arm and they walked briskly toward the stucco manse on flagstone weaving through a manicured landscape fringed with palm trees and punctuated by bursts of flowers.

I went out, the gate grinding shut behind me.

Then I looked at the note that Velda had passed me. *Pigalle, 9 tonite.*

CHAPTER EIGHT

The "World-Famous" Place Pigalle, just west of Collins Avenue, dressed up its undistinguished yellow-brick facade by writing its name in black letters outlined in pink neon and displaying movie-house-style posters of such top-name peelers as Tempest Storm and Dixie Evans.

But "The Fabulous 4D Gal" and "The Marilyn Monroe of Burlesk" were strictly Thanksgiving-to-Easter material. The rest of the year, the facade's boldly lettered guarantee of "15 Exotic Dancers 15" was honored by unknowns. Famous or novice, all take-it-off talent at the Pigalle was required A.K. ("After Kefauver") to put the brakes on at bras and g-strings.

I thought the gorgeous taffy-haired no-name doll sharing the stage with a Cuban combo was doing just fine, her bump-and-grind mixing well with Latin rhythms. She was a game kid, considering the place was barely a third full. Purplish lighting turned cigarette smoke into a garish haze while a handful of lone men got hustled for drinks at the bar by strippers who'd finished their sets. Despite the Cuban band, the place lived up to the Parisian promise of its name by way of Can-Can-Girl wall murals from some modestly talented but highly horny local Lautrec.

Velda was in a booth in the back, waiting, half of her highball gone. A lovely woman with midnight hair brushing mostly bare shoulders, the straight-across cut of her bangs echoing the horizontal neckline of the black sheath dress. Only about a third of her bosom was exposed. Just enough to turn my mouth as cottony as going off the booze.

"We don't have long," she said. No hello or other preamble. "Quinn is out on 'business' and didn't say what kind or when he'd return. I told that houseboy of his that I wanted to go shopping on Lincoln Road."

"You have a car to do that?"

"Quinn said I could drive his Jag when he was out. But I want to be there when he gets back. We shouldn't risk it for very long."

"Risk seeing each other, you mean."

She swallowed, nodded. Her eyes seemed only able to meet mine momentarily. "I don't suppose it will do any good to ask you to trust me? And to ask you again to just…"

"Go? No." I gave her the nasty grin. "The time to ask for my trust was right before you blew town. Of course, you did leave me that sweet kiss-off. 'Goodbye.' Yeah, that about covers everything."

A waitress in an Apache dancer getup came over and I ordered a beer.

Velda was looking at her folded hands. I expected tension in her face, and maybe I'd thought my little speech would make her cry. It hadn't quite. Her eyes glistened some, but her face had a softness that comes with resignation.

I said, "You want to tell me, or should I take a stab?"

"Go… go ahead." Her voice was small with some tremor. I'd never heard it like that.

I folded my arms, cocked my head. "I figure around four months ago, maybe five, your old boss Wade Manley approached you. He had an undercover assignment that needed doing, and he just *knew* that you were the only policewoman who might be up to it. Never mind that you weren't a policewoman anymore. That you had other things going on in your life right now. How am I doing?"

She nodded twice, still not looking at me. Sipped her highball.

I went on: "Nolly Quinn was a very nasty piece of work who had slipped through Manley's fingers back in the old days. A hugely successful call girl racket that the Big Man had never been able to shut down, and then Nolly gathered his bankroll and left. Well, that stuck in the Big Man's craw. Then years later, somehow your old boss got a line on what Nolly was up to now—specifically that he was setting up a major drug smuggling operation in Miami."

The Cuban combo was doing a big finish. The taffy-haired doll must have been down to her bra and g-string. Scattered applause and a few hoots and hollers seemed to confirm that.

"For some reason, Nolly was back in our town, the big town, probably to let interested parties know that he could supply quantities of certain products that they would be very much interested in merchandising. The Big Man moved fast, pulling you in, convincing you that this was a job that simply had to be done. Nolly is a notorious ladies' man, and that provided the perfect opportunity to get a man... that is, a *woman*... on the inside. He put you next to Quinn and let nature take its course."

She shivered. "You make it sound..."

"Like you ran around on me? And then ran out on me?"

My beer came.

She looked up and it was as if raising her head was lifting a thousand-pound weight. "Mike, this isn't just any undercover assignment. Nolly Quinn may look handsome and seem charming, but he's a killer many times over. When he was running that call girl operation, half a dozen women who crossed him disappeared. Just fell off the earth. Now, he's putting together a network importing drugs from only ninety miles away, a flow of misery that once started will be *impossible* to stop."

Something came out of me that pretended to be a laugh. "And all that's supposed to make me feel *better* about this? Velda, two recent valentines of Nolly's got massacred. A suicide and a hit-and-run. Did you *know* about that?"

She nodded, still only making occasional, momentary eye contact. "I… I knew going in. Mike, he has to be stopped."

"Let *me* stop him."

She shook her head and her eyes met mine for several seconds, a new record. "No. That's… that's one of the reasons I couldn't tell you what I was going to do, where I was going to go. Because you would solve the problem the Mike Hammer way, and this has to be done with evidence."

"Evidence is optional in my book."

A twitch of a smile flickered in the morose face. "Exactly. Look at what you've done since you hit town! You sent Quinn's top two boys to the emergency room. Then you stormed into that club and almost choked Quinn to death."

"Almost only counts in horse shoes," I muttered.

"Very funny, Mike. And believe me, I wouldn't mind watching you take him apart piece by piece. But there are two key players in this who I haven't identified yet. Silent partners, without whom we have nothing. And on top of that, I've been keeping track of all his contacts. I'm building a list of the plane pilots and boat captains he's using. I even have names of representatives of the

Cuban government he's in bed with."

"Oh yeah. We *definitely* want who he's in bed with."

Her eyes closed, two seconds passed, and they opened again. "That's the other reason, Mike. The reason why I couldn't tell you about any of this. Why you had to think that it was over between us... and maybe it *will* be anyway, but..."

"You said there was another reason."

"A detective of your skills hasn't deduced it?" She gave me a heartbroken, heartbreaking smile. "What would you have said if I told you I was going undercover to get as close as possible to a notorious ladies' man of a mobster?"

I didn't need to answer. We both knew.

She took a gulp of her highball. "And now... now this investigation has cost my old boss his life."

I made a fist and managed not to slam it onto the table. "That's right, it has. Your old boss is very goddamn dead. Making you an undercover agent without a superior to report to. That means it's time to pack up and leave, baby. In anybody's book."

Now she dared to hold my eyes. "That's Wade Manley you're talking about, Mike. Remember him? He put us together. Sure, you and I had met, you'd bailed me out of a jam... and blown my cover. But the Big Man looked at us, and maybe he saw a couple of people who were bruised and battered, and could tell what we might be able to do for each other. What we might *mean* for each other."

Now *I* couldn't look at *her*. "Well, he didn't hesitate in pulling you back in, and wrecking what we built."

"*Is* it wrecked, Mike?"

Could not goddamn look *at her.*

"Kitten… undercover is one thing. Under covers is another."

Her sigh began in Manhattan and came out in Miami Beach. "Mike, Mike… it's not that way. Quinn hasn't touched me. Well, he's *touched* me… he's kissed me…"

"Have fun?"

She made a face. "It's like kissing a mannequin. He doesn't have any real human feelings that I can see. Maybe greed and jealousy. What he really wants is a beautiful woman on his arm."

"I'm supposed to believe that."

"It's true. Oh, eventually he'll want more than kissing and… petting. He's very serious about me, Mike. He thinks I'm as smart as I am beautiful. That I'd make a great… partner in life."

"I'll position myself up front to catch the bridal bouquet."

She laughed a little, a horrible thing. "He's like you, Mike. Wants to save it for the honeymoon. Who would think a hound like him would be so old-fashioned? Who would think a hound like *you* would be so old-fashioned?"

I said nothing.

She finished her highball. "But that's not all of it. You see, he's got a dose, Mike. The good 'ol V.D. He's popping penicillin like M&M's. He doesn't want to take any risks that his 'baby' might catch it."

I frowned at her, something wiggling in the back of my head. "That cure takes weeks, not months."

Lightly she said, "I know, but he's paranoid about it. You can *see* how vain he is." Then she leaned forward and now she had no trouble looking right at me. "And I'm close, Mike. Very damn close."

I shrugged. "So you're close. Fine. Swell. But listen to me, doll—things are different now. *I'm* in this. You know it, and Nolly Quinn knows it. Putting you in harm's way was never my plan... but my presence here does that. *That* much you and your old boss were right about."

She sighed, nodded.

I leaned way forward, my voice so hushed God couldn't have overheard. "You need to promise me that you'll call me in if there's any sign of trouble."

With one hand she touched the sapphire ring on the other. "I will, Mike. I promise. I *will.*"

I gave her the number at the Sea Breeze.

"Just so you know," I said, "I'm legal down here. A pal of Pat's on the Miami P.D got me a temporary gun permit and a P.I. license."

That seemed to amuse her. "Well, I know what a stickler you are for the legal niceties."

It's not polite to point but that's what I did. "Things are changing, kitten. Ramping up. This afternoon a consortium of gangsters with legit business interests tried to hire me to kill Nolly Quinn."

"*What?*"

"They think things are too hot in Miami after Kefauver to risk opening up Cuba as a major drug connection right now. In addition, they consider Quinn a general pain in the ass. But killing him gangster-style puts them in a bad light with the Chamber of Commerce. So what better way to get rid of the preening jackass than to have a kill-crazy private eye from New York take him out?"

Her eyes were big, whites showing all around. "You didn't... you aren't *going* to..."

"You know better than that, kitten. I don't hire out my gun that way. I reserve it strictly for sport."

That got a smile out of her.

Then I pointed at her again. "But if your goal is to gather evidence, well, fine—I'll play that game for a few days, too. I'm going to investigate your shack-up pal, starting with those two girl friends he broke up with the hard way."

"You're in the right place to do it," she said.

"How's that?"

"The suicide used to work here."

I was gaping at her when she slipped out of the booth and leaned in and kissed my forehead. "For a drunk, Mike, you're slipping."

"Huh?"

"You haven't touched your beer."

And she was gone.

* * *

I followed up on Velda's lead immediately, though with limited results.

The bartender was new, and the first three strippers claimed not to remember Dotty Flynn. Since each dancer between sets was pursuing the time-honored B-girl role, this was turning into an expensive inquiry at $5 per brandy with Coke chaser. Funny how when the girls took a sip of brandy followed by one of Coke, the level of the Coke in the glass went up and not down.

That's how the suckers got drunk and the dolls stayed sober.

But finally that taffy-haired number who'd been stripping when I came in settled down beside me at the bar and got cooperative right away. We had no trouble talking because the first show was over and during the break an Oriental kid was at the ivories singing "La Mer" in French, piano-bar style.

"I remember Dotty," she said.

Under a trowel-worth of make-up, this brown-eyed kid with a perfect 36 chassis was about eighteen. She looked like the kind of prom date that made springing for a corsage a good investment.

"Dotty left maybe a week after I started here. That tall-dark-and-handsome daddy with the nightclub came in one night and spotted her and I guess liked what he saw. Next thing I heard, he hired her away to work his hatcheck concession."

"I'd think working here at the Pigalle would pay off better than that."

"Not really. I'd snap up a hatcheck gig at a place like that in a heartbeat. You get to keep more clothes on and the tips are steady." She nodded to her brandy and Coke on the bar next to where we sat. "Plus, you don't have to go through this dumb routine."

"What kind of outlook on life did Dotty have?"

She frowned and her forehead make-up cracked a little. "What do you mean, mister?"

"I mean, was she blue all the time or cheerful or just in between?"

"I didn't know her well, but she was a chipper gal. She liked people. Liked attention. But it can get old having strange men drooling on you, and older still that it's your job to do it. She was a good dancer. She'd done chorus line work in Vegas."

"So maybe she thought the hatcheck gig would lead to the chorus line at Nolly Q's?"

"Oh, yes. Matter of fact, that's what I heard—that she was told she'd be a floor-show dancer next winter. Next I knew, she's that Nolly guy's main squeeze. Then she *wasn't*, and… and later I saw the squib in the paper."

She shivered, and only a heel would notice what nice things that did for the pastie-tipped contents of her sheer bra.

I asked, "Did Dotty strike you as the kind of girl who could bounce back from a letdown? Or could you buy her opening her wrists?"

That made her go white around the throat where the make-up stopped. "I don't know, mister. I really don't. This isn't an easy life, working a town like this. But she wasn't who I would *expect* to take that way out."

I patted her arm and slipped her an extra fin.

Very quietly she leaned forward and whispered, "I'm off at two."

I leaned in and whispered, "I don't pay for it, sugar."

"Big guys like you never do. Maybe little girls like me like it that way."

"Maybe we'll test that theory another time."

That kid would rate a corsage any day.

On the way to the motel, I was looking at the pieces in front of me like some retiree sitting in the sun with a big jigsaw puzzle spread out on his glass-topped beachfront umbrella table. Still at the nothing-but-pieces stage, no picture emerging yet. The trouble was there were a couple of puzzles to put together, that overlapped and merged, or maybe didn't merge. The Manley kill. The dead ex-girl friends. The mobsters who wanted Nolly dead. The Cuban drug supply.

And a low-life lover boy who was living with a lovely woman, *my* woman, but not sharing his bed with her. If Velda was to be believed.

Plus things on the periphery that might or might not be missing puzzle pieces. I kept moving them around, trying to make things fit, hoping I wasn't like some kid who got his scissors out and starting cutting off this bit and that corner to make the pieces shove together…

Then as I approached the Sea Breeze, something jarred me from my thoughts.

The NO VACANCY part of the rooftop neon was glowing red, like the exit sign in a theater. This was odd because, ever since I'd checked in anyway, Duff had never left the sign on at all after ten o'clock. It was odder still because if there was one thing the Sea Breeze had, it was vacancies.

I slowed a little and went on by. The Sea Breeze did appear to have one new guest—parked down from Duff's own vehicle was a recent-model two-tone Packard, white up top and blue below. Clashing with an orange Florida license plate.

I cruised on to a gas station separated from the motel by an overgrown lot, and pulled in. The station was closed. I left the Ford there and walked back. The night was clear and a nearly full moon made an ivory searchlight. It was cool but humid.

The room the Packard was parked near was dark. But no lights were on anywhere in the place, including the Duffys' living quarters above the office.

I listened at the door and windows of what might be the room belonging to the Packard, and heard nothing. Checking the vehicle, I came up with something interesting—it was unlocked. *The keys were in it.* Either somebody was careless, or somebody wanted it ready and waiting. To hop in and go.

After doing what?

The auto registration said Elmer Johnson and the

address was Tampa. Did somebody from Florida think this was a good time of year to check into the Sea Breeze? Maybe. Price was right. But what could you do off-season in Miami that you couldn't do just as well in Tampa?

Salesman, maybe. Probably I was making something out of nothing. I got out my .45.

When I entered the office, I reached up with my left to silence the bell over the door. No sign of disturbance, but a too-familiar coppery smell was in the air. I didn't turn on the light but gently kicked the door wider to let in a broader shaft of moonlight, more of which was already streaking in the front windows.

Then I caught it.

Feet were sticking out from behind the registration desk. Four feet. In sandals. A male pair. A female pair.

In a clumsy embrace where they had been dumped were Merle and Martha Duffy, casual in their summery attire. His friendly ugly mug was looking right at her, though of course he wasn't seeing anything. Nor was his plump, pretty wife, her blue eyes glassy.

Each had been shot in the head, probably with a .22 automatic. That's what contract killers usually preferred.

Of course, the Duffys weren't the intended victims. They were just what the military calls non-combatant casualties.

Sorry, Duffy, I said in my head. *But I promise you they'll go out worse.*

On the wall of keys above the corpses, the hook for

my unit was empty. Somebody had my spare. Every other pair of keys hung in place, meaning the Packard party hadn't checked in at all. Why should they? They were in *another* room, weren't they? My room.

Waiting.

I thought for a few seconds about what to do. The Packard's keys were in it. Maybe I should climb in and start 'er up and drive around back, picking up some nice speed and crash it on through into my unit. Anybody who didn't get smashed by the vehicle I could shoot.

But I didn't know if the Duffys had any kids they'd be leaving the place to, or if they had insurance either, so that seemed a little on the reckless side.

Or I could go around and smash a window and take pot luck. Too bad I didn't have a shotgun handy because I could blow a hole in the wall from the next-door unit and make a good old-fashioned turkey shoot of it. Using my key in the door was no go, because they would hear it, and even coming in fast and blasting, I might catch some lead. And kicking the door down was risky, even with flimsy wood like that, because you never know how many kicks it's going to take. Kicking down doors wasn't as easy as in the movies.

Then I remembered something I'd noticed when I was hanging my suits in my closet. I reached across the Duffys to the wall of keys and plucked one off: the key to the room on the highway side of the motel that shared a back wall with my unit on the ocean side.

I went outside and down to that room and entered

quietly, leaving the light off though I probably could have turned it on. Still, even the click of a light switch might warn them.

And "them" was right: I could hear two muffled voices, talking casually, conversationally, not loud, but these were paper-thin walls. One was higher pitched, meaning it wasn't just one talker droning on. That was good that they were chatting over there. Meant they were over-confident. Always a plus having the other side cocky.

I snugged the .45 back under my arm. I took the change from my pockets and my car keys too and set them soundlessly down on the dresser.

Very slowly and carefully, I opened the closet door, leaning in and glancing up to confirm I had remembered right.

I had.

Then I went over and got the chair from the little writing desk and set it in place within the closet, so quiet, so careful. I stepped up on the chair. It creaked just a tad. I froze. Above me was the hardboard panel to the crawl space. I pushed it up and to one side. It made only a whisper of a sound.

The tricky part was to lift myself up and over without making a racket. The result wasn't silent by any means, but the conversation, which you could hear better up here, didn't stop, so they probably hadn't heard anything.

Now I was in the crawl space. Nothing much up

here, not the ductwork you would find up north or the insulation, either. Just electrical access. Nothing stored up here, which was helpful. I had a good clear path to where the closet in my room was, but edging over without attracting attention meant taking it very slow and easy.

On my belly like I was crawling across the jungle floor from one foxhole to another, I inched along until I came to the recessed panel in the floor above my closet. The panel was not designed to be lifted out from above. Maybe the pair waiting below in my room would think it was mice or rats up here, if they heard the tiny sounds. Couldn't be helped. My fingernails worked to catch the lip of the hardboard panel from its wooden frame, but they just wouldn't catch, they wouldn't catch, *goddamnit*, they just wouldn't…

…then they did.

I lifted the hardboard square carefully up and out and set it down to one side.

I took a second to mentally refresh myself of the room's layout. From where I was positioned, the closet was in the front-left corner next to the can. The bed was on the west wall, which would be at my right. The door was on the east wall, way over to my left, if one of my new friends was waiting there to catch me coming in.

I got the .45 back out, which would make it tougher to ease myself down gracefully, but I wouldn't want to have to take time to pull it, so somewhat awkwardly

I lowered myself to the closet floor. They were still talking out there. Not loud. Something about bets they'd laid on a Tampa Smokers ball game, which struck me as just plain sad. Particularly for a last conversation.

I turned the knob, shouldered the door open and the big guy in a hideous floral yellow-and-orange sport shirt sitting at the end of my bed with a .22 auto in his mitt swung a stupid thick-lipped face my way just in time to see the yellow-and-orange tongue of flame from the snout of the roaring rod try to lick him like a friendly hound. His head stayed in one piece but everything in it beat a hasty, splattery retreat onto the far wall. He slid off the floor with a thump as the guy positioned by the door, skinny and crew-cut with a sliver of a face, yelped in wide-eyed surprise and blasted one my way with a .22.

I was already hitting the deck where his thick-lipped dead partner on the floor looked at me with an even stupider expression than in life. In the meantime, his tall skinny partner was out the door. I got up and across the room, pausing at one side of the opening, peeking out before making a clay pigeon of myself.

What I saw was the back of him, as he disappeared into the stand of palm trees and tropical flowers and brush just beyond the rear of the motel. I went after him fast, but moments upon entering the mini-jungle the sound of him on the move, twigs snapping, fronds flapping, leaves scraping each other like sandpaper, suddenly ceased. Somewhere in here he was waiting for me, to pick me off.

I grinned, hefting the .45 even as I crouched. This was a game I'd played before. Jungle warfare? Fine by me. Dense as the greenery was, enough moonlight filtered in for me to see the most distinct, foliage-free route out, which was to my left. Staying low, each movement calculated, each step measured, I made my way through the patch of palms and flora.

Before getting to the beach, I let go with four rapid-fire shots spaced a few feet apart, their thunder rolling through the trees and brush like the threat of a storm, stirring and shaking and shattering branches and leaves, and my adversary gave up his position as he moved noisily, heedlessly out of the underbrush toward the beach. My .45 followed him, booming off three more shots.

I was slamming in a fresh clip when I emerged from the thicket but this time he'd outsmarted me, he was waiting on his belly down in the gently sloping sand with that .22 steadied by a second hand, as if on a firing range.

But I pitched to one side before his shots snapped into the night, only I hit hard and off-balance and the .45 flew from my fingers. He kept firing, but I was less a target now, and then he was out of ammo and clambered up. I was on my feet, too, grinning at him, my hands clawed before me.

He froze there in the moonlight for half a second, feet on sand, moon-tipped water to his back, deciding whether to reload or run. He was a gangly guy, in another of those floral shirts with chinos, and sandals like Duffy and his wife had worn. The killer's face had angles including a sharp chin and he had an Ichabod Crane look to him.

He chose flight, first tossing his gun at me and missing wide, then moving to where the sand was damp but not spongy, because it was faster under foot than the dry variety, and with those legs, those churning legs, he was making headway, arms pumping. Down the beach were the lights of civilization. But this was the jungle.

He was fueled by fear and I was powered by rage, and rage trumps fear every time. I closed the distance and then closed it some more and threw a tackle at him and brought him down, his landing a hard, bone-crunching one that sent a chest worth of air whooshing out of him.

He was gulping for breath as I dragged him by the ankles into the water and then he was squirming, trying to get away, like a flopping fish on a boat deck. I suppose I should have questioned him about who sent him, but my brain was filled with a burning blood-red image of the Duffys in their final embrace behind the desk of their happy little business. I moved farther into the lazy lapping water, dragging him with me, and he was splashing and fighting all the way. He was so damn tall that I had to go in to my shoulders as I held him upside down, clutching him around the waist, my arms completely submerged, his arms too flailing under there, his legs and feet above me, kicking, kicking, kicking, for the longest time.

Until they stopped.

Then I hauled him out of there, first by the waist and then by the ankles again and made a concave snail trail in the sand as I dragged him back into the stand of palms, just to get him out of the way. The moonlight guided me as I looked for and found my .45, and I went over and collected his .22, too. Then I went back and with my feet covered up the gouge his towed body had made in the beach.

I went into my room where the other gunman lay with his head still draining like a badly cracked egg. I gathered everything of mine, packing the duffel, putting the suits back in their clothing bag, all of that. Dragged a chair over to get up there and replace the hardwood panel in the crawlspace access. For what good it might do, I wiped off everything I'd touched. Or anyway that I remembered touching.

I did the same in the room where I'd entered the crawlspace, putting everything back in place but not bothering climbing back up there, and collecting my change and car keys. I wiped down the office door knob and a place where I'd leaned against the counter. I tore the page from the guest register that had my name on it.

Then I returned to the gas station, lugging both duffel and suit carrier, and drove till I found a phone booth. I used the slip of paper in my pocket to get a certain number. Surprisingly, Bonetti himself answered.

"Mr. Bonetti, Mike Hammer. Think you could clean up a little mess I made?"

CHAPTER NINE

I woke just before nine a.m. from a deep sleep that left me with no residue of dreams, though I knew damn well there had been some. Incidents like last night brought combat memories bubbling up out of the subconscious ooze and my bed sheets were twisted and damp with fever-dream sweat, even with the air-conditioning blasting.

This was the Raleigh Hotel on Collins Avenue, not one of the newer monoliths but another of those prewar modern affairs, seven floors of white wedding cake with the corners rounded off. The room was shades of yellow from sunflower to mustard with seaweed green drapes, with furnishings that were either coolly modern or coldly so, depending on your taste. To me it was icy, but I was glad to have any roof over my head that wasn't the charnel house the Sea Breeze Motel had become.

Sunshine filtered through filmy inner drapes, but I still had to switch on the nightstand lamp to see the phone and its list of in-house numbers better. I ordered up a room service breakfast of scrambled eggs, American fries, grits, pancakes and crisp bacon with a pitcher of coffee plus milk and sugar. Apparently I'd built up an appetite, thanks to last night's fun and games.

Waiting for the chow, I showered, the wheels and gears in my brain slowly starting to grind and whir, then quickly picking up speed. In this relentless mechanical way the pieces that I'd so rationally tried to put in place last night finally assembled themselves unbidden.

Suddenly I understood why Nolly Quinn went through dolls like paper napkins. Knew at once why it was so important for him to seem like a cross between Casanova and Errol Flynn, always a stunning babe on his arm. Now I got why the women came and went, only maybe they didn't come at all. Maybe they found out his secret.

Nolly Quinn was queer!

That had to be it. No guy with factory wiring could shack up with a sensuous female like Velda and not lay a glove on her. Emotions flowed through me in a rush, like fuel seeking an engine—relief, hope, even a giddy euphoria that had me laughing out loud as I toweled myself off.

Nolly Quinn thought he'd found in Velda a woman not only beautiful but so very smart and shrewd that he could trust her with his secret. A woman as grasping as he was who would even marry him, becoming the ultimate beard, sharing with him the luxurious wealth and ease that his corrupt business dealings would bring.

And marital union would be just another corrupt business deal. After all, the best way for a homosexual like Nolly to hide was in plain sight, with a beautiful woman beside him.

But did Velda know?

She'd shown no indication that she did. Of course lately she'd been holding her cards close to that lovely chest of hers. Maybe like Nolly, she was safeguarding the Big Secret—for now.

What a *burden* he'd had, all these years, keeping his real self secret from the hard-case crowd he ran with. If those Italian and Sicilian mobsters had ever learned they had a "fanook" among them, doing business with them, dealing with their inner circle, Nolly Quinn would be instantly marked for murder. And his mentor Mandy Meyers—upon discovering that the gifted protégé he'd been backing for so many years was nothing but a dirty "fegelah"—would rush to take the sting off himself and rubber-stamp Nolly's death warrant.

The lousy hypocritical shits.

Who were these bastards to sit in judgment of anybody? They lived and breathed and thrived on theft and murder, on the degradation of women, the intimidation of the weak, the marketing of human suffering. But what some guy did behind closed bedroom doors made them sick, offended their gentle sensitive souls, so he has got to die.

And it wouldn't be pretty.

They'd torture him slowly with fist and fire and blade and blunt instrument and before breath left him they would wind up by cutting off his manhood and for public humiliation stuff the private parts in his mouth and leave his battered, carved-up, cigarette-burned body in the trunk of a stolen car somewhere. Unlocked, so that the terrible lesson they'd taught Nolly Quinn would spread far and wide among others of his reviled kind.

The irony of course was that Quinn, for all his efforts to appear a man among men, had already angered his Mafia associates to the point where for all his successes, they wanted him dead right now, for their own venal reasons. None having a damn thing to do with his sexual bent.

Had Nolly's two dead ex-girl friends learned his secret, and paid the highest price? Had they seen past his blather about taking a V.D. cure or waiting till the honeymoon?

It fit, it fit, every goddamn piece fit, finally slipping into place.

Yet it was just a theory, wasn't it? Nothing but a glorified hunch cooked up in the shower. But hell— that cigarette holder alone should have been enough! Or his name in pink neon. Come on! And that houseboy—was he a live-in lover, also hiding in plain sight? A wife to do the cleaning and dishes and laundry and provide other services, when Nolly's current arm candy wasn't around?

I had to be right!

But I didn't have enough, and when I *did* have enough, what the hell would I do with it?

No, for now Nolly's secret had to be my secret, too. Until I knew without doubt it was true. And knew what to do when I did.

I was half-way through breakfast when Alberto Bonetti called. He would be at the hotel in fifteen minutes. Should I come down to him? No, he'd come up to me.

So with my breakfast dishes on a tray in the hall, I dragged a metal-and-cushions chair over to face the metal-and-cushions couch that hugged a windowed wall and paralleled the nearby side of my bed. This was no suite, like that patriotic number at the Betsy. I had a hunch a lot of Miami Beach hotel rooms were like this—functional, modern, not spacious at all.

I was dressed in a tan lightweight suit, jacket unbuttoned, my .45 under my arm, its weight oddly comforting.

I wasn't expecting anything—after all, wasn't Bonetti in his way a captain of industry? But back in his salad days, he had "disappeared" people for Lucky Luciano, and even now he had a legion of modern-day Romans ready to kill at a nod or a thumbs-down glance.

His knock came soft, almost tentative.

When I answered the door, I again saw a future retiree in casual vacation dress, palm-pattern cream-colored sport shirt, baggy tan pants, and brown Italian loafers. No sandals with socks for Alberto Bonetti.

Also no bodyguards. He had come alone, and I hadn't even insisted on it. Really I couldn't insist on anything, under the circumstances; as much as I hated it, I was in his debt. It started with this hotel that he'd directed me to last night, which he either had money in or did enough business with to order up no-questions-asked five-star service.

"Good morning, Mr. Hammer," Bonetti said through the mild smile forming in the mass of grooves and cracks that were his dark-eyed face.

His slicked salt-and-pepper hair was immaculate, though the thick black eyebrows could use a trim. He smelled of Old Spice. So did I. We were brothers in aftershave.

This time the mob boss did extend a hand, and it was like somebody handed me a ham. Yet he didn't overdo the grip. Firm, no-nonsense, but that's all.

I stood to one side, gesturing him into my little temporary castle, and he said as he entered, "You look rested."

"Slept like a stone."

"Some people wouldn't, after last night."

I shrugged. "Just another day at the office."

That seemed to amuse him a little. I waved to the couch and he sat. I plopped down opposite him, hands in my lap. Folding my arms would be a defensive gesture, and this was a man I had to meet head on, eye to eye.

Still looking vaguely amused, he asked, "Do you feel you really need that hardware, Mr. Hammer?"

He meant the .45. It wasn't that my tailors had let me down—the gun was easily seen with my suit coat hanging open. I'd wanted it that way.

I said, "Recent events indicate I just might."

He didn't argue the point.

As if the meeting had now come to order, he said, "You checked in here two days ago. You only stayed at the Sea Breeze one night." He might have been filling in an amnesiac. "Just that first night—should anybody ask, which they might not."

"I paid cash when I checked in," I said, "and ripped the page I signed from the guest registry on my way out."

"Good." His big thick hands were folded just above his slight paunch. "What happened at the Sea Breeze was one of these pointless, useless tragedies that you hear about sometimes. A lovely couple who ran a motel brutally slain by person or persons unknown, who also emptied the cash box. Mr. Duffy a war veteran who served in the European theater, and Mrs. Duffy a retired third-grade school teacher. Grown son and daughter. All of this will be in the Miami *News* this afternoon."

"What about the *Herald*?"

He shook his head. "The information did not become available in time for the morning papers. Maybe tomorrow."

"I'll check it out. I try to stay current with *Little Orphan Annie*, anyway."

This time no amusement registered. "You expressed a concern last night, about Captain Pell of the Detective Bureau. That he knows you were a guest at the Sea Breeze. Your stay there being limited to one night should take care of that. But it may not become an issue anyway, as it's not a Miami P.D. case."

I frowned. "Why no Miami cops?"

"It's a matter for the sheriff's department. The Sea Breeze rests in a strip of unincorporated land. Of course, the different police departments exchange information, and there's some interdepartmental discussion. That's to be expected in this case, since the murdering thieves got away."

"Oh they did?"

"Yes, and I have my doubts that they'll ever turn up." He shifted on the couch; it didn't look any more comfortable than my chair. "And as for those two friends of yours, Mr. Hammer, from that party of yours that got out of hand? Those gentlemen from Tampa? They were anxious to go deep sea fishing in the moonlight. Wanting to be accommodating, my people took them out a very long way. They had the time of their lives and in fact are still out there now."

"Thoughtful of you."

"As for the after-party mess in your motel room, it really didn't amount to much. Some routine clean-up. Soap and water. Patch and paint two small holes in facing walls. The car the gents from Tampa left behind should be spare parts by now. And you'll be glad to know your festivities didn't disturb any of the neighbors. No one in the area called the police with a noise complaint. Nice of them, wouldn't you say?"

"Swell." I shifted in my uncomfy seat. "I, uh... I appreciate this, Mr. Bonetti."

His smile was small but there was something sinister in it, and his eyes had disappeared into slits that lived in pouches of flesh, like a lizard's.

"Do you, Mr. Hammer? That's generous of you to say, considering how you obviously feel about my 'line of business,' as you put it the other day. You remember—when you were turning down our money?"

I'd had just about enough of this bastard but I did my best not to show it. "I *do* appreciate it."

He smiled like an Italian Buddha. "Good. I know you hate having to come to us, Mr. Hammer, to *me*... but the truth is, we're not that different, you and I."

The smile vanished, the well-grooved face blank yet somehow threatening.

"You think, Mr. Hammer, that you're on some kind of higher moral plain than we are, but you're not. Not by some distance. You use the very same kind of methods that we do."

I gave him an Irish Buddha grin. "I think of it as fighting fire with fire."

His eyes were half-placid, half-dead. "Think of it how you like, Mr. Hammer. You said you'd handle the Nolly Quinn matter for us without remuneration... 'on the house.' But if you are under the impression that this gives you the leeway to walk away should the mood strike you, let me remind you—what I did for you last night, and today, changes that. Cleaning up at the Sea Breeze, and finding you a room in another hotel, a discreet hotel, *that* is your down payment for the Quinn contract. Never mind that briefcase you turned your nose up at. *Got* that, Mr. Hammer?"

Part of me admired the old mobster for how he'd handled this. Part of me wanted to throw him out the window. We were on the sixth floor so that would have done the trick.

But all I said was, "Got it, Mr. Bonetti."

"Good." He patted his knees like a department store Santa summoning another kid. "By the way, you're comped here at the Raleigh, meals and parking and dry cleaning and whatever." He got up, turned to go, but then looked back at me. *Right* at me. "Any time-table on handling the Quinn thing?"

"No," I said. "But I won't try your patience."

He flashed a crocodile grin. "I don't care what anybody says, Mr. Hammer—you're a smart man."

We did not shake hands a second time, but he nodded a little on his way out. I didn't.

I went over and used the phone.

I needed to deal with another problem: Ben Sauer at the *Herald* knew I'd been staying at the Sea Breeze, too.

And I would hate for him to put *that* in his paper...

* * *

Even at its opening time of eleven a.m., the Raleigh bar was an intimate, wood-paneled study in subdued lighting. Just beyond the curve of the bar and its white-jacketed black-tie bartender, under a wall of signed celebrity photos, were a couple of red leather booths.

I was in one of them, sitting across from the Miami *Herald*'s city editor. When I ordered his namesake whiskey sour for him, he warned me he only had fifteen minutes to spare. And then later, when a second whiskey sour went on my tab, he reminded me again.

I sipped at my pilsner of beer and said, "I talked to a stripper pal of Dorothy Flynn's. She didn't think much of the suicide angle."

Today Sauer's suspenders were orange. Fitting for a Florida newsman giving a Bronx cheer. "Both those deaths smell to high heaven, Mike, and you damn well know it."

But for the bartender, we had the place to ourselves.

"They stink," I agreed. "But that's an opinion. I'd rather *know* it. Can you help me out?"

The horsey face formed a rumpled grin. "How would you like to talk to another stripper?"

"Beats city editors." Particularly whiskey-for-breakfast ones.

He leaned closer, as if afraid non-existent fellow patrons might hear. "Turns out the hit-and-run victim, Kimberly Carter—before her affair with Nolly Quinn—was employed at the Five O'Clock Club."

I frowned. "Think I've heard of that place."

"You probably have. The Five is the classiest and longest running of the Beach stripperies. Martha Raye owns the joint, but she doesn't appear there off-season."

"Since when is Martha Raye a stripteaser?"

He chuckled. "Well, of course she's not... but neither was the Carter girl. The Five O'Clock is an old-fashioned burly-cue show straight out of Minsky. A blackout sketch or musical number between every strip *artiste*."

"Kim Carter didn't peel?"

"No, Mike—gal was strictly a songbird, although a genuine beauty, features like Gene Tierney, body like Jane Russell."

"The kind of female who just might attract Nolly Quinn's attention."

"No 'might' about it. Anyway, one of my guys tracked down a pal of the Carter girl's at the Five, Miranda Storsky from Minnesota, stripping under the name Randi Storm. She even bunked with Carter for a while, back when they were both working there."

"Is Randi Storm still at the Five?"

"Still at the Five." He gulped a little whiskey sour and then grinned, eyes glittering. "And this is where Jolson says, 'You ain't heard nothin' yet.' Get this—*Miss Storm* was hooked up with Nolly Quinn for a time herself."

The back of my neck prickled and I sat forward. "We already knew one of Quinn's cast-off's was a stripper. Did the Storm girl come before or after Kim Carter on the Quinn roster?"

He turned up his hands. "No idea. What I gave you is what I got, Mike. Which is as far as my guy could take it."

"Why?"

He raised a finger for me to wait, took a slow sip of whiskey sour. "Because Miss Storm wanted *dough* to talk. A paper like the *Herald* doesn't pay for stories, Mike. You know that. Once you set that precedent, you're screwed."

He leaned over confidentially again.

"But," he said, "there's no reason a private snoop can't slip a little cash to a source. I mean, that's a time-honored tradition, right? And, Mike? From what I hear about Miss Randi Storm, you might want to slip her more than cash."

I shook my head, smiled in a *give-me-a-break* way. "I'm not looking for a new girl, Ben. I'm trying to get my old one back."

He gestured around him with two hands, one with the drink in it. "Well, that's all well and good, Michael, but in the meantime, there are plenty of substitute sweethearts in Miami Beach."

Even though the bar was empty.

I bulled on. "What about that ex of Quinn's who's supposed to be working as a waitress somewhere?"

He nodded quickly. "A little redhead named Erin Valen. Fashion magazine type, supposed to be a real stunner, sometime model, sometime chorus girl. Used to wait tables at Leon and Eddie's, former gay spot now strip joint, post-Kefauver. But she's not there now."

The delicate green-eyed face flashed into my mind. "Ben, *that's* the girl I told you about—the one who confronted Nolly at his club. The doll he slapped and got himself belted by me."

His eyebrows were up. "She'd sure as hell be worth talking to."

"You got a number or address on her?"

"Might be I could get that for you." The corners of his mouth went up and so did his eyebrows. "*If* you have something for me."

Till now, he'd seemed a little drunk—unlikely for a gentleman drinker who knew how to imbibe all day and not show it. Playing me maybe. This time when he leaned forward, he seemed stone-cold sober.

He said, "Listen, Mike. I've unloaded for you. Now how about unloading for me?"

I gave him my best innocent look, which isn't great. "Any particular subject, Ben?"

He raised his chin as if tempting me to tag him. "There was a double homicide at the Sea Breeze Motel last night. The proprietor and his old lady. The till was empty, drawer open. Let me ask you something, if you're not too much of a big-city boy to know such esoteric things... who bothers sticking up a motel in the boondocks during the off-season?"

"You got me. A dope maybe?"

He finished off the whiskey sour with a gulp, then shook his head. "No. No, Mike, it may have something to *do* with dope… but no. You were staying at the Sea Breeze, Mike. You told me so."

I shrugged. "I was there a single night, Ben. Then I moved here to the Raleigh. Check with the desk."

"Why do I think I needn't bother?" His eyes were narrow and his smile was wide. "You want me to believe that it's just a coincidence that Mike Hammer, notorious conveyor of violence and frontier justice, checked into a motel where two violent deaths occurred shortly thereafter? Two deaths that just happened to happen when this self-same Hammer character is in town, rattling the cage of one of Miami Beach's most notorious underworld figures?"

"The way you say it," I said, "it sounds like there might be a story in it."

"Doesn't there just?"

I had another sip of beer. "But if I were you, Ben, I wouldn't waste my time on some smalltime robbery/homicide at the Sea Breeze."

"Oh you wouldn't?"

"No." I grinned at him. "I'd try to stay on the good side of a guy who can deliver you an exclusive on something much bigger—as long as that guy doesn't get sidetracked and dragged down because of that other, smaller story."

"Say a measly robbery/homicide."

"Say that." I saluted him with the pilsner, then drank a little more. "But it's up to you, chum. You might start by putting me in touch with that girl Erin."

"See what I can do."

"Another whiskey sour before you go?"

He thought about that for a fraction of a second. "Sure," he said. "Why not?"

She was in a lime-green sundress with a yellow silk scarf at her throat and darker green wedgies that showed off her red-nailed toes. The colors went well with all that red hair. Her make-up was still a little heavy but her features retained a delicate prettiness in daylight, though the almond-shaped green eyes were hiding behind sunglasses.

I had sunglasses on, too. I was in a blue seascape sport shirt and dark blue bathing trunks and leather sandals, all purchased in the Raleigh gift shop and charged to my room.

We were seated poolside in deck chairs near a bar that resided under a squat white ersatz lighthouse that despite its hanging red life buoys looked more like a cement toadstool. We were near the diving board of an enormous curlicue-shaped pool, though no one was swimming right now, not even Esther Williams. A few loungers were after sun. Honeymooners again. The ubiquitous retiree couples lurked on the periphery at tables under umbrellas.

Mostly, though, we were alone, just us and the carefully planted palm trees. Even the white sand beach beyond was uncluttered with humans, and the ocean and sky seemed just painted backdrops in a movie. The sun was hot but the humidity had backed off and the warmth felt oddly healing.

She had called my room, where I was keeping my head down till dark, saying she'd heard I wanted to talk to her. And she offered to come to me. That's what I call service.

Now Erin Valen was next to me drinking a Sidecar and I was on my second beer of the day.

"Sure, I talked to Nolly about both of those girls," she said, her voice tinged with that improbable mix of naive and knowing. She shook her head. "Those poor dead girls. Nolly said they'd both been very nice kids and he was sorry they'd been... he put it so poetically... touched by tragedy."

There was nothing poetic about the way that hit-and-run driver had touched Kimberly Carter. Or how a razor blade had touched Dorothy Flynn's wrists.

I asked, "You broke up with him recently?"

She nodded. Sullen resentment hardened her voice: "After he took up with that big dark-haired Viking."

I probed gently. "Were you around when he was doing business with people?"

She shook her head vigorously but the red hair refused to tousle. "Not at all. We went to the club a lot, and to other nightspots. It was during the season and he took me to Copa City and the Latin Quarter and the Vagabonds. I got to see so many big-name stars."

"Sounds like he liked to show you off."

The thin lovely lips formed a smile of mildly chagrined pride. "I guess he must have. He did seem to like having me on his arm. But you know, we stayed in a lot, too. We were at his house much of the time. Beautiful place—have you seen it?"

"Just from the outside."

"There's a fantastic pool, so much privacy."

"Do you mind my asking why you broke up?"

She frowned and there was a quiver in her chin and her voice too when she said, "That *woman* broke us up. That damn Viking he brought back from Manhattan with him."

"You don't like her much."

She shrugged with her face. "I never met her really. I just… hate her on general principles, I guess. But… I'm sorry. I forget. She was your *girl*, right?"

"Far as I'm concerned, she still is."

A smile blossomed. "You gonna do the caveman bit and drag her back to Manhattan?"

"It's within the realm of possibility."

She sighed, the smile fading. "Wish I could help. I really wish I could help."

"Erin, would you answer a very personal question for me?"

"Well… I don't know. Maybe you better just ask and see."

I leaned over and touched her hand. Gently. I made my voice gentle, too. "You were intimate with Quinn, right? You slept with him?"

She looked away. Drew her hand away, as well. I wished I could see the green eyes under the sunglasses right now because her face was otherwise as immobile as a porcelain doll's.

Now her voice drew tight. "That *is* very personal, isn't it, Mike?"

I thought it would be less than gallant of me to mention what her hand had done in my lap in the Nolly Q's parking lot.

"There's a reason," I said.

She sipped the Sidecar. "Nolly has… a condition he's taking medicine for."

"You mean V.D."

Her face swung to me sharply. "How do *you* know about that?"

"I just do."

"We… we fooled around. He's normal, if that's what you mean. He's a big handsome guy, and it's no surprise some lowlife female gave him a, you know, a dose." Her face clenched with sincerity. "But this isn't about sex, Mike. It's about love. You *do* know there's a difference?"

I shrugged. "They're usually intertwined in a man and woman."

"You love that… what's her name?"

"Velda."

"Someday, if you marry Velda, you'll be old. Her, too. You might not be interested in… doing it any more."

I grinned. "Erin, I doubt I'll ever be *that* old."

She grinned back. "It happens to the best stallion on

the stud farm, Mike. Don't kid yourself. Someday the sex will be gone, but love needs to still be there. Love is so important, Mike. And I just know that Nolly is a good man at heart. A loving man at heart."

This was not an argument worth getting into, because I would never win. Reminding her, if she even knew, that Quinn had been a Murder Incorporated killer in his teens seemed unkind. But a man could do a lot worse than having a girl like Erin love him.

She was studying me, squinting as if trying to bring me into focus. "You're a *detective*, aren't you? Police?"

"No. Private. But I'm not on a case, really. This is personal, Erin."

Her face was as sad as it was pretty, and it was very pretty. "This is about your girl. Velda. Lovely name, I'll give her that. You have a room here?"

"I do."

Her smile went one-sided and wicked or anyway naughty. "I still think we should get back at them. You want to go up there and just… fool around a little?"

"No, honey. I've got it too bad for that."

"Really carrying the torch for that Viking, huh?"

"Afraid so."

"Pity." She got up, gathered her little purse, and leaned over and kissed my cheek.

"See, you big galoot," she said, eyes sparkling. "I was right. It really *is* about love not sex."

And then she walked toward the hotel, getting yearning looks from guys on honeymoons with their beautiful unaware dolls on their tummies sunbathing. Sex was always in there somewhere.

CHAPTER TEN

With its mission lines and cathedral windows, the white two-story Five O'Clock Club might have been a chapel. But in the neon noon of night, on Twentieth just off the oceanfront hotel row of Collins Avenue, the glass-brick entryway under a rounded marquee said the worshipers here were late-night types not Sunday morning. Above it all loomed not God, but a big round neon sign with a clock set permanently to five encircled by glowing letters spelling out the club's name.

The classy nightspot look held on inside, with nothing that immediately said it was Miami Beach's longest-running strip joint—hatcheck stand, bouncers in tuxes playing greeter, a decor of cool greens and warm red-browns accented with white, a low-key ambience courtesy of hidden lighting. The fully stocked bar along one side was overseen by a bartender in white jacket and black tie, and bordered by walls bearing photos of Martha Raye and also of Bob Hope, Bing Crosby and other showbiz luminaries, although always with Raye in the shot.

It was unlikely any but the comedienne co-owner of the place ever appeared on a stage where right now Joe E. Ross and Dave Starr were doing a very blue version of the old "Slowly I turned" routine.

The crowd couldn't really be called that, just a sprinkling of men alone and a couple of couples at linen-cloth-covered tables, mostly near the stage by a postage-stamp dance floor. As at the Pigalle, strippers between sets were circulating, operating as B-girls, though a shade more decorously dressed here in flowing sheer nightgowns over bras and g-strings.

A waiter in a tux earned a buck for seating me in a booth, then an eye blink later a tawny-tressed cocktail waitress came over. She was a pug-nose cutie in a little ruffled sparkly blue thing that started half-way down her bosom and stopped where her mesh stockings began. She asked what I wanted.

"Is that a trick question?" I grinned at her.

"Would I trick you?" she said ambiguously, smiling back. Maybe she thought I was a card. Or maybe she had mouths to feed at home. A kid or two or probably some no-good louse.

"I'll have a beer," I said.

She gave me some options and I picked one, then asked, "Has Randi Storm been on yet?"

"She's about to start her last set," she said, nodding toward the stage where Dave Starr was belting Joe E. Ross with a battered hat. "But don't worry—she mixes with the customers for a while after that."

"Thanks, honey."

She scurried off.

A small, formerly handsome M.C. in an obvious toupee came quickly out, grabbed the microphone like Sinatra at the Paramount and said, "You think *those* guys are crazy, you should see my brother! He thinks he's a chicken. I'd talk him out of it, but I need the eggs."

Nobody laughed except himself, and a honeymooner-type couple got up and started out. He hollered at them, saying, "Wait a minute, kids, wait a minute!" The couple lingered as he rushed off stage and came back with a pair of black rubbers on a serving tray. "You might need these!"

The couple made a face and went out, but there was a muffled laugh somewhere in back.

In triumph, the M.C. tossed his props into the wings, gripped the mike and went on to say how proud the Five O'Clock Club was to present "the very stormy, oh so *randy*, Miss Randi *Storm!*"

Soon the little upstage combo, drums, guitar, bass and sax, was belting out "Stormy Weather" as a tall doll hipped it on draped in a midnight blue gown so tight her belly button showed.

Randi Storm née Miranda Storsky was, like a rose, a genuine beauty by any name. Honey-blonde hair, big blue eyes, a full lush mouth, the kind of farm girl good looks that Hollywood loves to remake as glamour. The distribution of her hourglass figure put plenty of sand up top, so much so that she made my cute waitress look like a boy.

The doll kept time just fine but with a misstep here and there, never quite stumbling. Not that any man here would have given a damn, but Randi Storm seemed a little clumsy up there.

No, not clumsy. *Tipsy.*

It took her eight minutes plus increasingly up-tempo arrangements of "Moonglow," "Harlem Nocturne" and "Temptation" to get down to the legal limit of sheer bra, pasties and g-string. I had already passed a fin to the waitress to direct Miss Storm in my direction when her B-girl duties began.

Her act marked the end of the show and the M.C. said another would start in half an hour. The combo played dance music in case anybody was interested, which they weren't.

Before long Randi Storm came sashaying over to my booth in a sheer blue nightgown, overdoing the hip action, though there are worse sins. She had a little blue beaded purse along. I nodded and smiled, half-rising, and she got in on my side of the booth. She sat nice and close.

Miss Storm wasn't drunk but she sure wasn't sober. And closer up, that farm-girl mug of hers showed lines around the eyes, a not-so milk-fed complexion, and vertical smoker's creases above the lush lips. She was either older than she otherwise looked or had lived a very tough life for a kid from Minnesota.

"I guess you know I'm Randi," she purred throatily. Double entendre seemed to be the preferred strategy of babes here at the Five O'Clock.

"I'm Mike," I said and we shook hands, hers angled at the wrist in somebody's idea of elegance. "Shall we order some champagne?"

She beamed so broad she cracked her make-up. "Why, you must be a mind-reader, Mike."

The waitress came over and suddenly the brandy and chaser routine at the Pigalle seemed like a bargain. Champagne was thirty-six bucks for a bottle with a "Don" Pérignon label. Our pug-nosed server poured us both a glass and stuffed the bottle back in the ice bucket beside Miss Storm.

"Bottoms up," she said, naturally, and we toasted, but I didn't drink mine. Just set it down. She emptied her glass and handed me the bottle to pour her some more.

Sticking to her script, she said, "You know why this place is called the Five O'Clock, sweetie? There's a free round served at five p.m. Used to be one at five a.m., too, till the blue laws came in."

This girl had a problem that I knew all too well. The standard B-girl routine with champagne was to pour most if not all of each glass into the ice bucket when the male who bought it was busy looking at her tits. Like the spitting routine with the brandy and

Coke chaser, this kept the doll sober and got the guy lubricated to a proper fool-and-his-money condition.

Unless I missed my guess, Randi Storm had been drinking through her entire shift. That she wasn't drunk on her pretty behind only meant that her champagne guzzling had been periodically interrupted by dance sets where on stage she sweat out some of the alcohol.

Damn. Ever since I went off the sauce, it seemed like everybody around me was a lush. But at this point I had no desire for the stuff, and felt pity for this bosomy babe who was letting booze and cheap champagne speed up her aging process.

She got in the purse and withdrew a deck of Luckies, selected one and I took her lighter from her and fired her up, my hand shaking just slightly. Smoke was drifting in here like San Francisco fog before dawn, making me a little nauseous; so was the smoke of her Lucky.

"So, Mike," she said, with a boozer's compensating over-enunciation, "you sound like an East Coast boy. *Are* you an East Coast boy?"

"New York. Manhattan born and bred, dollface."

She sucked at her cigarette, leaving red in her wake. "I woulda bet Brooklyn. What brings you to town, handsome?"

Time to cut through the mundane chatter.

"Which do you prefer, baby," I said, smiling at her through the blue-gray cloud she was making, "Miranda or Randi?"

She frowned and thought about sliding out of the

booth, but I grabbed her arm. Not hard. She started to protest and I said, "Stick around. There might be some dough in it."

She thought about that.

I encouraged her some more: "I'm not a hood, baby."

"Then… then you're a *cop*."

I nodded, adding, "But the private variety."

Still frowning, she said, "For real? Not some New York snowbird working on one of these candy-ass departments around here? Didn't transfer or anything?"

"No. I'm in town on a job."

She shook her head hard enough to rattle. "You have the *wrong* gal, pal. I don't hook on the side or anything, so if it's a wife looking to get the goods on her—"

"I don't handle divorce cases."

"*All* private dicks handle divorce cases."

I didn't argue the point. "I want to talk to you about Nolly Quinn. A contact at the *Herald* said you know things."

For a moment it froze her. Then a grin grew that had been revamped in recent years from an innocent farm girl's into a hardened city broad's.

"Did your guy at the *Herald* tell you," she said, lowering her voice, "that I'm not some lending library? That you gotta pay premium rates for what I know?"

I nodded. "Like I said, there's some dough in it."

She wasn't whispering exactly but I had to work to hear over the combo. "You said 'might' be some dough, Mike. There could be *no* 'might' about this. Nolly Quinn is a dangerous dude. You better know that, if you're sniffing around about him. Don't let his slick front fool you."

"You were with Quinn for how long?"

"Around two months. That's a good long time for our wandering boy."

I looked at her hard. "Time enough maybe, for you to see things, and learn things?"

She poured her own champagne this round and drank half a glass of the swill before she looked right back at me, eyes half-lidded in a combination of shrewdness and intoxication. "That's a nice name, Mike. I like it. You look like you might be nice."

"No 'might' about it, baby. I'm a sweetheart."

"Miranda."

"Huh?"

"I prefer Miranda. That's what my girl friends call me. Might be nice to hear a man say it. But I like the name Randi fine for, you know, a stage name. It's sexy. And Storm, well that says something."

Right. It said she was trying to steal Tempest Storm's thunder.

She gestured with her sloshing champagne glass. "You look like a rough apple, Mike, but I can feel it. That you're a nice guy. I'm good about such things. Sensing stuff. Judge of character is what I am. Good judge. Of character."

She finished the glass and was getting herself

another when I held her wrist.

"Let's back off on that stuff," I said, "till we've talked this out."

"Talked what out?"

"You tell me."

She leaned close and raised a wavery finger to her lips. "Gonna *cost* you."

"I can give you a hundred right now, doll. A nice crisp C-note."

She shook her head. "No, I need *real* money, Mike. This is big. This'll make big, big ripples for Nolly, if it gets out. A guy in his racket can get killed for something like this. A girl can get killed for telling it."

"What kind of money are we talking, Miranda?"

"I want ten grand."

I reared back as if somebody had fired a shot my way. "That's a lot of money, honey."

"I need ten grand to get out of this town and start over somewhere. I might even go home, Mike. There was a guy back there, big football star, high school football star. But he was too damn dumb to get a scholarship to college. He's running his daddy's furniture store now. Well, his daddy's still running it, but he's the manager, so-called. And I thought it was small potatoes. Just small little potatoes. I wanted to be in show business, I was pretty and I could dance, and wouldn't you know it won two beauty contests, and I went to New York but wound up here in Miami, and I'm starting to think I took a wrong turn, Mike. A really wrong turn."

"Going back to Minnesota sounds like a good move."

She snorted a laugh. "Somebody at the *Herald* really gave you a bunch of stuff on me, didn't they? But never mind me, Mike. Here's the thing. Nolly's got a secret. A *big* secret. If it gets out, those gangsters he does business with will kill him dead. Deader than a doornail dead."

I hated to break it to her, but I said, "Baby, I already *know* Nolly's secret."

"Do you now, Mike? Then what is it?"

"He's queer."

She shook her head. "No. That's not it."

I blinked away the surprise of that response, saying, "I think it is. He never had sex with you, did he? Or any of those women he paraded around on his arm like a Rolex watch? He gave you a song and dance about being on penicillin for the clap, or wanting to wait till the honeymoon. Right?"

The stripper was shaking her head, smiling just a little, amused. "Wrong. I had sex with Nolly plenty of times, Mike. So did Dotty Flynn, who was my roommate, when she was with him. We both agreed that he stunk in the sack, like a lot of too-handsome Romeos. But if you think he didn't have sex with girls, you are missing the boat." She emphasized every syllable with a nod: "*Miss*-ing the *gol*-durn *boat*."

I let her pour herself another glass of the cheap champagne. My head was swirling worse than hers had to be. If Nolly wasn't gay, then what the hell was his secret? What did Miranda alias Randi know about the bastard that I didn't? That wasn't common knowledge?

"Miranda, do you think your friend Dotty was murdered?"

She nodded emphatically. "Yes. Oh yes, yes, yes. Cut herself in the tub? Never. No way never."

"Did she know this… this secret of Nolly's?"

"Yes."

"Did it have to do with his business?"

"Yes."

Is it bigger than a bread box?

"Goddamnit, woman, what is his damn *secret*? Is it the identity of his two silent partners? That's *it*, isn't it? Do you know which of the five Mafia families in New York is planning to do business with him on this Cuban thing?"

That at least got her attention. "You *have* been digging, haven't you, Mike?"

"Is that it? Is *that* what you have to sell?"

She opened her palm and she tapped a red-nailed finger in it. "Right here. Cross Madame Miranda's palm with ten thousand clams and she will tell all."

The waitress came over and asked, "More champagne?"

"No!" I snapped.

And the waitress moved away quickly, looking hurt.

Miss Storm was pouring herself the last half of a glass the bottle held. She probably wouldn't have hit the bubbly this hard if she hadn't already danced her last set. Or maybe the subject matter of Nolly Quinn gave her a thirst.

I thought about it. Ten grand was not something I could lay hands on easily, especially down here, and who could say that what she knew was worth the asking price?

But I could *feel* it, the answer to everything was sitting across from me, inside a babe with a great body and beautiful face and eyes working to stay open.

"I think I can get you that ten gees," I said.

Her eyelids rolled back like startled window shades. "You can? Goodie!"

"You're done here for the night, right?"

She nodded.

"Then go back to your dressing room and get your street clothes on. I have to make a phone call. Meet me up front."

"I knew you'd come through for me, handsome." She waved like a little kid. "Bye bye!"

Then she hip-swayed across the room, weaving between tables and heading through the diaphanous curtain of cigarette smoke to the stage door at the back. A lot of male eyes followed her. Even drunk she was something to behold.

There was a pay phone on the wall by the men's room up near the hatcheck window. I used the phone number Alberto Bonetti gave me, hoping he'd be in. It was only ten-thirty but maybe these middle-aged types went to bed early, even mob boss ones.

The Betsy Ross Hotel switchboard put me through to his room. A rough male voice answered, a bodyguard probably, but soon Bonetti was on the line.

I said, "Do you think you could arrange a ten-thousand dollar pay-off for a source with key information about Nolly Quinn?"

He was gruff but businesslike. "What kind of information, Mr. Hammer?"

"I think this source knows who Nolly's silent partners are. One could be his contact with a rival family back home. The other is probably a local politician or maybe somebody on the Cuba end."

"That *would* be worth ten grand."

"A bargain for you fellas, considering I walked away from one-hundred-thousand."

He chuckled. "Still thinking about that, Mr. Hammer? Dreaming about the long green you turned your nose up at?"

"I don't give a damn about your money, Bonetti. I'd pay this source myself but I don't have the cash. This is your call."

He didn't hesitate: "Make the deal. I can have the cash for you yet tonight if need be."

"That might help. My source is a little on the sloshed side right now, and at a later, more sober moment might decide either to ask for more or not talk at all."

"Take the source to your hotel room and call me from there when you're in. I'll messenger the cash over."

"Okay," I said, and we hung up.

I waited another ten minutes for her, and almost didn't recognize her when she walked up to me in the vestibule with all that honey hair up and no make-up. She was in a sleeveless sundress as red as a stop light, but her figure alone would halt traffic.

"You look pretty," I said.

"Thanks. What now, Mike?"

"Now we go to my hotel room."

Only vaguely tipsy, she said, "This is a little sudden, isn't it?"

I grinned at her. "Honey, I just arranged to get you ten grand for what you know. You can decide how to best express your gratitude later."

"All right," she said, and she leaned close to me. She smelled good, some kind of Parisian perfume probably, and the champagne hadn't screwed up her breath. "But, Mike—you don't get to know what *I* know, till I get the cash. Hate to be mercenary, but a girl's gotta look after herself in this cold old world."

I just smiled and shook my head, and held the door open for her. She was still in front of me, just beyond the overhang, when the black Cadillac slowed and from the rear driver's side window came the hand with a silenced automatic in it that coughed twice, spitting orange flame.

I was half-way to the cement, no time even to pull my .45, tugging her down with me, when the car roared off and people were yelling and screaming and then

I was cradling the girl from Minnesota in my arms at the entry to the chapel-like nightclub. The bullets had punctured her breasts, one each, two small puckers only slightly darker red than the sundress, but the back of her was torn and ragged and draining blood fast.

She looked so goddamn young and fresh and not at all drunk when she gazed up at me with the damnedest glazed smile and said, "*Mike...* bye... bye..."

"Goodbye, Miranda," I said, but she was already gone.

One uniformed cop took my basic information while the other one held back any bystanders. The plainclothes guys from the Miami Beach P.D. got there maybe ten minutes after the shooting. They went inside and took names and released all the patrons as well as the entertainers and the staff, asking only the manager to stick around.

I was detained of course. So were two men who'd been about to enter the Five O'Clock Club and a honeymooning couple who'd just exited. Nobody caught the license number, because the plate wore a mud smear like a mask.

The ambulance guys arrived, established the girl was dead in their brilliance and cooled their heels till the lab boys and photographers showed.

I kept my story simple and factual, as far as it went. I was down from New York, with proper licensing credentials, looking into the Miami end of a cop killing. Nolly Quinn was suspected to have been behind it and I was talking to known associates of his, including the late Randi Storm, who was an ex-Quinn girl friend. Miss Storm and I were leaving the strip club to seek quieter surroundings to talk. A shooter in a back seat window of a black Caddie had leaned out and fired twice with a silenced gun. I didn't see anything really but a hand with an automatic. A .22, I believed.

I knew this would take a while. Figured I would probably have to go to their station house and repeat my story ad infinitum till dawn anyway. But when I mentioned Captain Barney Pell had arranged my temporary local P.I. license and gun permit, they called him.

He showed in twenty minutes, took the lead detective aside and talked to him like a priest, gesturing toward me occasionally.

The night was humid and warm and Pell was sweating, the white shirt under his suit coat sopping. That didn't stop him from smoking a cigar. He had a supply, after all. The ambulance boys were loading the wicker basket with the dead girl in it when Pell slipped an arm around my shoulder and walked me back into the club.

We stood just inside the door.

His blue eyes were hooded and his smile was lopsided, but the effect of his bulb-nosed, lightly freckled face was somehow reassuring. He put a hand on my shoulder. Friendly not threatening.

"You really know how to have a good time in a vacation spot, don't you, Mike?"

Did he know about the Sea Breeze Motel?

"I have a ball everywhere I go, Barney. So—boy or girl?"

He beamed. "Boy! Bernard Jr. Man, Connie is over the moon about this thing. I mean, she had a rough ride, one of the longest damn labors in the history of that hospital. But she can't get the smile off her face, lookin' at the little one in her arms."

"I'm happy for you, Barney."

"You should try it. Haul that honey of yours home and keep her barefoot and pregnant."

Somehow that didn't sound a lot like Velda.

Grinning, he patted his suit coat where I keep my .45. "Sure you don't want a cigar?"

"No. I stopped smoking."

"And you stopped drinking. You *did* stop, Mike, didn't you?"

"I did, Barney. Nothing but a few beers a day."

He gave me a once-over glance. "You do look better. For a guy who just ducked some bullets, anyway. So what's the straight story here?"

I shrugged. "What I told the Miami Beach boys. This girl was an ex of Quinn's, who lived with him a while. And she was good friends with the Flynn girl who slit her wrists. And I wanted to talk to her about all that. I got interrupted."

Pell's face grew somber and a little disgusted. "It's

looking like Mr. Quinn is collecting a lot of dead girl friends lately. Some hobby."

"I'm close to nailing him, Barney, if this thing tonight doesn't slow me down."

He stuck his cigar back in his face and thought about it. "I'll talk to the Miami Beach boys. See if I can get you a pass on this. But you can't leave town. You still at that motel?"

Damn!

"No, Barney, I was just there for that first night. Couldn't see staying out in the sticks when the investigation centered here in Miami Beach. Moved to the Raleigh." I gestured in the hotel's direction.

He nodded, apparently accepting that.

"Let me see what I can do," he said. Then he reached in his inside suit coat pocket and got out a cellophane-wrapped "*It's-a-boy!*" cigar and dangled it in front of me. "Sure you don't want one? You don't have to inhale."

I took it. "I'll take one home to Pat Chambers for you."

That widened his grin. "You do that."

Then he went out to talk to his counterpart on the Miami Beach department.

I didn't remind him that one of Nolly Quinn's two cars was a black Cadillac.

In my hotel room, I put a long-distance call through

to Pat Chambers. I tried his apartment first and got him there.

"You sound sober enough," he said.

"I am sober. And if I'd been drunk, what happened tonight would have sobered me up."

I filled him in on the shooting at the Five O'Clock Club.

Pat said, "Nice that Barney could vouch for you with the Miami Beach P.D."

"Nice doesn't cover it. I was afraid your pal Barney would ask me some embarrassing questions about certain other things."

"Such as?"

"Yeah, like I'm going to tell you. Let's just say I was glad all he can talk about at the moment is that new baby of his. And his proud missus."

"Tell me about it," Pat chuckled. "At the police convention, he was passing out premature cigars all around the Waldorf ballroom."

"Well, he gave me another one for you." I shifted gears. "Getting anywhere on the guy seen talking to Manley the night he was killed?"

. Frustration hung on his voice like wet laundry. "I handled that myself, Mike, like I said I would, with help from some of my top people. I'd like to say we got something, but it's really so much air."

"Nobody got a good look at the guy?"

"They noticed him, that's all. We talked to sailors and hookers and dockworkers and truckers and barflies. They all say the same thing—big guy, but not too big. Heavy guy, but not fat. Dark hair, but not too dark. In his thirties maybe. Or his forties. Or maybe fifties. We brought the three most credible types in for the sketch artist. We got three drawings that looked nothing like each other of somebody that could have been anybody."

"Hell. It's the eye-witness curse—'He was medium.'"

"The only thing close to a lead that came of it is the guy was wearing a suit, tie and hat."

"Well, that narrows it down to four or five million."

"Including you and me, Mike. But it *is* suggestive. Think about it."

I did. "You mean, the patrons at Dirty Dick's are not exactly the suit-and-tie type."

"No. Whoever Wade Manley was talking with was not your usual patron of a waterfront dive."

"It's something, anyway. Where do you take it from here?"

He sighed. "Widening the canvass area. Wading through Manley's files for arrests of individuals who might hold a grudge. Pretty damn standard stuff. You think you've got anything?"

"I thought I did." I told him my theory that Nolly Quinn was a closeted homosexual using beautiful women as beards to protect himself from the disgusted wrath of his criminal cronies. And told Pat, too, how the dead stripper had shot that theory down, talking of some *other* secret of Nolly Quinn's.

"I figure she had the identities of Quinn's silent partners," I said.

"Makes sense. You may not have this one solved yet, but it sounds like the perfect Mike Hammer case."

"Yeah?"

"Chasing down all the clues at strip joints. But you know, if Nolly *were* gay, your stripper tour would make sense. It's like he was trolling those clubs for beautiful women to cast as make-believe girl friends."

"I didn't know her long, Pat, but that stripper Randi Storm… Miranda Storsky… was a nice enough kid. She just got mixed up with the wrong people."

"Sounds greedy to me."

"She wanted enough money to get out and start over. Who can fault her for that? Damnit, Pat, it's making me sick, this wholesale killing."

"It always does, when you aren't doing it."

But that wasn't funny, not to me.

We talked a while more, and he was relieved to learn that Velda had been on an undercover assignment for Manley all along.

"We really *are* working two ends of the same case," he said. "But, Mike—you have to pull her out of there. This Quinn character is bad news all the way. You can't let Velda be his *next* dead girl friend—fake or not."

Pat was right and I told him so.

We hung up.

I was flopped in a chair trying to decide whether to hit the rack or gather the energy to do what my buddy had suggested, and just go over to that bastard Quinn's fancy digs and drag Velda the hell out of there. *What was I waiting for?* Hadn't Nolly proven to be worth killing?

A knock came at the door and I was almost there when a male voice said, "Mr. Hammer—Mr. Bonetti sent us to check on you. Are you all right?"

Shit, I thought. I forgot to call Bonetti back and tell him what happened at the Five O'Clock Club. That the ten-thousand dollar pay-off plan had died with a farm girl from Minnesota.

The peephole showed me two big guys in sport coats and slacks who I recognized as two of the bodyguards who'd been lounging in the Betsy bar while I was having my talk with their bosses.

Just the same, I took the .45 out when I opened the door.

But before I could use it, hands gripped my arms on either side and a small bottle was uncorked to let the vapors of what must have been chloroform rise up into my face, into my mouth and up my nostrils, the reflexive intake of breath doing their work for them, and I was out.

CHAPTER ELEVEN

They were drunk-walking me down a dock, a big hulking shadow on either side of me, the tops of my shoes dragging and bumping over the planks. The back of my head felt damp and the chances were they'd sapped me after the genie in the chloroform bottle had given them their wish.

That stuff doesn't keep you out long, unless you really held a soaked rag to a guy's face. But that would likely kill him and certainly burn his skin to hell. So the tap on the skull would have been the clincher.

The headache I was waking to was no worse than the mother of all hangovers and likely a combination of chloroform after-effect and concussion. My hearing was muted, my limbs numb, my eyesight a blur. More gifts from the chemical genie.

I had vague near-memories of being lugged down

endless flights of back stairs and tossed in a waiting car's back seat and shoved face down on the floor where my arms were jerked behind me and bound tight together at the wrists. Of two male voices sounding far away yet right here, talking but not in conversation, sporadic bursts of speech over a ride that took fifteen minutes or an hour or all night.

Turn right.

Here?

No next one.

Watch *him* not me!

What d'you think I'm doing?

Might be faking.

It's the second left.

They say he's dangerous.

No, not there, next one.

Where it says Dinner Key?

Yeah that's it, that's the one, right there.

Even now I hadn't come completely around and for a while I sensed more than I saw as they pulled me along the dock. The night was cool, the humidity negligible. Gulls were calling to each other. Moored boats of various sizes were on either side of us, mostly dark but a few bigger craft emitted muffled music and distant chatter and laughter. The world seemed otherwise quiet, slumbering, the loudest sound the creak of timber under the size twelves of my captors.

My lungs were hungry and the sharp tang of sea air fed them and helped wake me further, though I kept my eyes slitted and my body limp, which was no effort at all. These big lumbering dark shadows were dragging me to my death, I knew that, yet I found the sound of water lapping at dock pilings strangely soothing.

Up ahead a small dark-complected mustached man in white from sneakers to captain's hat seemed almost to glow in the night. Well, not *all* in white—he had a black-holstered revolver low on his hip like a TV cowboy. Heel of a hand on the holstered gun butt, our captain was waiting for us beside a big powerboat, white hull, dark-wood cabin, green trim. Forty-some feet, maybe fifty. It would take two engines to power that beauty. You could have a whale of a fishing trip on it.

Or haul a hell of a cargo of contraband.

They held my limp frame up with big hands under my arms, like I was a prize fish they were displaying. Nothing but my wrists were bound and they hadn't bothered gagging me. If I made a sound they'd finish me. And the civilians on these boats, families among them, the giddy fun-seekers on the yachts, would die if they got involved. That I knew, too. These kind of men were not new to me. I was, in my way, one of them.

I knew even before they dragged me over and onto the deck and hauled me through the cabin and dumped me against the back wall of the cramped little galley that this was a one-way ride, like the "deep sea fishing trip" those dead guys at the motel got taken on by Bonetti's people.

Were these *Bonetti's people?*

Whoever they were, these kind of men didn't cruise out onto the ocean to have a quiet place to talk to you or even to torture you, unless they were in the mood or had the need. And I didn't have anything to tell them, no special knowledge for them to beat or burn out of me, no.

This was a disposal run.

The two big men in sport coats and slacks left me on the galley floor in a pile and moved through the cabin and out onto the rear deck. They cast off and as we rumbled out to sea, they sat out on those swivel chairs sports fishermen use.

My vision was back, although as far as my captors knew I was still out. They were definitely two of the bodyguards from the Betsy Hotel bar, but which mob boss they belonged to was a mystery that I could only dream of living to solve.

They were the kind of big men who had gotten so muscularly over-developed that their heads looked too small for their bodies. One had a light brown flattop and a baby face. The other had a dark brown butch and a flat nose. Both had killer tans. That they worked out and probably ate wheat germ didn't stop them from smoking. The ember eyes of their cigarettes glowed in the darkness like distant lights. They seemed in a pleasant mood.

Who doesn't like a relaxing outing?

I could catch much of their conversation despite

the engine purr and water rush because they were talking loud so they could hear each other up over the combined noise.

The baby-face flattop guy said, "You know that babe from Hialeah I been seeing?"

"The waitress with the water wings?"

"Yeah! Cute kid, great body, but also? She has got one smart mouth. *Always* the back talk. *Always* with the opinions."

"I hate that crap."

"Tell me about it. A nice rack only goes so far, you know? But I think I come up with the cure."

"Yeah?"

"She give me some lip last night and I just hauled off and belted her one."

"*Slapped* her?"

"No, I mean really clipped her one. On the chin. Lemme tell you, the dame's got a glass jaw. She went down like…" But he couldn't think of anything to compare it to, and just added, "…right away."

His pal got a good laugh out of that. "Man, I wanna be *you* when I grow up! You know what's wrong with me and my approach to the cooze?"

"No. Educate me."

"I am too damn nice for my own damn good. I am just a big softie with these broads. I'm ashamed to say it, but the most I ever done with a lippy skirt was slap her around some. And it never seems to do no good."

"Well, you gotta really *belt* her one. Give her

something to think about. Something to look at in the mirror for a while. You'll thank me."

"Man, you are a genius. You oughta patent this stuff."

Flattop and Flatnose, ladies and gentlemen. Catch them between strippers at the Five O'Clock Club.

By this time we'd been cruising for five minutes or so, and I had come fully around. I still had the headache but it had backed off into a dull throb and the numbness of my extremities had faded. My vision was clear and my hearing sharp. I was alert in the way only a man fighting for his life experiences.

For several minutes I'd been feeling at the ropes binding my wrists together. I was lucky—it wasn't heavy rope, nothing boating grade, and it wasn't nylon either or anything coated. Just good old-fashioned two-strand fiber stuff.

What God's-two-gifts-to-women out there didn't know was that I'd been hauled off before by goons who had tied my hands behind me. After I managed to live through it the first time, I got smart and started taking precautions. Like carrying a safety-razor blade in a slit of my belt in back. This required dexterity and patience, because if I fumbled the blade while trying to slip it out of its hiding place, or dropped the thing while using it to saw through the rope, it could hop out of reach. Worse, it might attract attention.

And even with simple two-strand fiber rope, carving away at it with a three-fingered backward grip was a tedious, frustrating, lengthy, awkward damn process.

I was just starting to make some headway when Flattop asked his pal, "There any beers in the galley fridge?"

I froze.

"I dunno," Flatnose said. "Suppose I could check."

"Don't suppose it, *do* it… Hey, watch the bucket! Don't trip over that thing! Hell of a mess if you do."

"Could be worse."

"Yeah?"

"I could kick it!"

Let's hear it for them, ladies and gentlemen.

Flatnose moved quickly through the cabin, got to the galley's doorless doorway and paused there to look down at me. Then he stepped in and bent down in front of me.

Was he going to check on my bonds?

I could feel his eyes on me, crawling on me like bugs. My chin was on my chest and I was giving every appearance of still being out cold or anyway thought I was. He shrugged a little, then turned on his bent legs to get in the small fridge under the counter.

If I'd had the ropes loose, it would have been perfect. I could have kicked him in the head and pulled the .38 stuck in his belt and shot his buddy through the open door onto the deck and then finished him and climbed the ladder to the flybridge and drilled that damn Cuban captain.

But I was only half-way through the rope. And at least Flatnose wasn't checking me—a closer look and I'd be royally screwed.

"*No beer!*" he called.

"Cheap bastard we work for!"

Flatnose ambled back through the cabin to his chair out on the rear deck. "Well, hell, we *are* working. You know the boss don't like drinking on the job."

"Beer ain't drinking. Beer is just socializing."

I didn't disagree.

With no beer to socialize them, they seemed to have run out of conversation. They just sat out there enjoying the cool evening, two fishermen without poles.

We had to be out far enough for them to get rid of me. Why the long boat ride? Not that I was complaining…

I kept sawing away with the blade, hoping it didn't get dull or break on me, and then finally, *yes*, the rope gave way and my wrists were free.

The question was—*now what?*

I could rush out there with the advantage of surprise but they were big guys with guns, and up on the flybridge at the wheel was that little Cuban captain with his revolver.

And me with my trusty razor blade.

Okay, surprise and a razor blade, but brawny armed bastards backed up by a Cuban cowboy with a heater just *might* give them the advantage on me…

Quietly I got to my feet. The galley made such cramped quarters that I could put one hand on the electric stove and the other on the sink counter. Carefully, as soundlessly as possible, I started opening drawers and looking into them. This was a kitchen, wasn't it? Wouldn't there be knives? Didn't there *have* to be knives?

And there were knives, all right, in the first drawer I tried—and spoons and forks. Maybe I could butter these bastards to death, only I didn't have any butter.

My hands did most of the work as my eyes stayed as much as possible on the two muscle-heads out on deck, chatting again now, lighting up fresh smokes, their backs to me, but glancing at each other occasionally, but should one of them out of the corner of an eye catch a glimpse of me on my feet rifling the galley, the guns would come out in full force.

I could always hurl silverware at them.

So I kept opening drawers, which at least cooperated by not scraping or squeaking or causing any clatter of contents. The second drawer gave me towels, goddamn towels, and the third drawer served up hot pads, and the fourth spatulas and measuring spoons and cups and a church key. Maybe the cabinets would have canned goods. A hard-flung can of beans was better than hurling handfuls of silverware, anyway.

Out on deck, the conversation had come around to me.

"I don't *get* this," Flattop said.

"What don't you get?" Flatnose asked.

"Why don't we just put a bullet in the son of a bitch, one behind the ear, pow, and toss his ass over the side?"

"The boss said what he wanted and that's exactly how we're gonna do it."

"But *why*? It can't be safe, attractin' those damn things. And *I* ain't handling that bucket. Hell no. I say bump him, tell the boss we done it just like he asked, the guy died real hard and terrible and everything, you should have seen the blood, boss, and go on about our merry way."

"Not worth risking. Captain Pedro and the boss are tight, remember. He'll rat us out."

"Why don't we slip Pedro a fin?"

"Naw. It's Hammer who's gonna get slipped the fin."

That made them both start laughing, really hard. It had a hollow sound in the night.

Flatnose's ice-breaker joke was enough to make Flattop cave in.

"All right all right! We'll go along with the boss's wishes! It's his stupid boat."

I wasn't loving the sound of any of this, and then the fifth drawer came slowly open and I hit pay dirt.

Knives.

Not the silverware variety, but the real stainless steel things, sharp and to the point. The multiple blades reflected a slivered image of my grinning face back at me. Half a dozen beautiful knives, and the one I chose over the bigger carving knife seemed fitting as hell to me.

I shut the drawer and resumed my position on the floor against the back wall.

I was still in my suit coat, so the knife wouldn't show slipped in my waistband at the left, cross-draw style.

Forcing the grin off my face, I looped the rope around my wrists and held it in place with my fingers.

The captain was slowing the engines. We hadn't come to a stop, but our speed was cut way down.

What was going on?

And what the hell were those two muscle-bound idiots doing *out there?*

Flatnose had work gloves on, the handle of a good-size bucket in one hand and some kind of metal scoop in the other. He stood at the stern, close to the edge of the boat, leaning out, tossing scoopfuls of something into the water, making little splashes.

Then I caught glimmers of red in midair before bits and pieces dropped into the sea.

Bloody chum.

Flatnose did this a number of times, and finally yelled, "The damn bucket's empty! *You* see anything?"

Flattop said, "No… no. Not a goddamn thing. Wait! *There!* Oh hell, *there!*"

Flatnose backed away and put the bucket down, tossing the scoop into it with a clunk. "Pedro! *Stop!* Cut the engines!"

The motors eased to a stop and the steady slosh seemed suddenly very loud, the boat bobbing on the water, no longer cutting through it.

Flatnose tore off his gloves and tossed them in the bucket, too, and said, "Let's get him. Get this stupid thing over with."

I lowered my head, played dead. If I didn't handle this

just right, very soon I wouldn't be playing at anything.

They clomped through the cabin and both of the big men looked very pale. Shit, these guys were scared shitless, and not of me. Not by a long shot.

A sinking feeling at the pit of my stomach said I already knew why these tough guys seemed about to piss themselves.

As they dragged me onto the deck to the stern, I saw the dark fins, four of them, no five, cutting calmly through water that would have been as black as they were had the waves not been touched by the ivory of a full moon and a sky clustered with stars. Gracefully the fins glided, nothing deadly apparent about them at all, just a sweeping beauty, Nature's majesty at work, and as both men gaped at the sight, each with a hand holding onto an arm of mine, they hesitated for a moment, horror-struck by what they were about to do, what they were about to witness, hard men made momentarily soft by fear, and my right arm came around and my hand found the fileting knife in my waistband and it came sweeping out to cut a wide swath of ragged red across Flattop's throat. His eyes were large and so was his open mouth, but nothing came out, and I couldn't resist giving him a left on the chin that sent him over the side where two fins swooped in to argue over a meal.

A startled Flatnose was panicky but not enough so that he didn't go for his gun, only I sank the knife in deep before he could get his hands on the weapon and I cut him open with several sharp turns and twists of the blade, and when I shoved him over, grabbing his

.38 revolver from his belt with my left hand as I did, his guts were hanging out of him like tentacles, but he wasn't dead, not yet, so I like to think he heard me say, "So long, chum!"

Behind me the brutal ballet continued as I turned the weapon onto Pedro up on the flybridge. He was goggling at me, the wheel of the bobbing boat at his back, his hands nowhere near the holstered weapon. "I'm just the captain! I'm just the captain!"

"What, did you blink and miss the mutiny?" I asked. "*I'm* the captain."

"Yes, sir!"

"Now take that gun by two fingers and toss it overboard."

Then he did something very stupid. When he had the gun out, he suffered an attack of cowboy courage and shifted the weapon into a full grip and bared his teeth and aimed at me. He never got to fire.

My bullet shattered his smile on its way through him and out of the back of his head. He tumbled off the flybridge, taking some hard bumps on the ride down to the deck that he probably didn't feel.

Damn.

I would rather have kept Pedro alive. I understood very well that he was as much a part of this murder party as the late muscle boys, and seeing him go did not choke me up any. But now there was nobody to identify "the boss," the man who had dictated my death by shark.

I tossed the ex-captain over, too, keeping his gun.

At the back and on either side of the boat, the waters were churning and splashing and frothing and foaming as the ivory highlights on the black ocean turned scarlet. Two of them fought over a big chunk of somebody, then one pulled away with it and made a submarine dive. Bits and pieces of the two men were floating and now and then a black-eyed white-faced jagged-toothed head would emerge to snap it up like a dog for a biscuit, then disappear under the choppy blackness.

Miami Beach was just a vague twinkling of lights, and I was no sailor. But the sharks were bumping up against the hull, wanting more biscuits, and I could handle a motorboat, so I figured I could make my way home.

CHAPTER TWELVE

My .45 was on the floor just inside the hotel-room door, where the invitation by chloroform vapor had made me drop it. I picked the gun up, holstered it out of habit, thinking about collecting my things and checking out of the Raleigh, but right now whoever had commissioned that pleasure cruise figured I wasn't a problem anymore.

So for the time being, this room was safe. Or so, in my frazzled state of mind, I convinced myself.

It was almost one-thirty in the morning and Mrs. Hammer's little boy had had a busy day. The hotel bed was a temptress beckoning me, and for the first time since I'd kicked the stuff the idea of a drink before beddy-bye sounded damn good to me. I sat on the edge of the bed and picked up the nightstand phone with room service in mind and then gave the hotel operator

Alberto Bonetti's number at the Betsy instead.

"This had better be important, Mr. Hammer," came a growl worthy of a caged grizzly poked with a stick.

"Somebody just tried to kill me. Went to great lengths to try in fact. I thought you might like to know. Unless you already did."

"*What* the hell—"

"Gather up your pals in the Kefauver Fan Club and meet me in the bar at the Betsy just after closing. Civella, Meyers, De Luca, the whole lovely bunch. I want everybody there or you can find somebody else to take care of your Nolly Quinn problem."

"Damnit, man, you expect me to round up important men like *that* in the middle of the night to—"

"To get a timely report from the private eye they hired, yeah. You're my clients, after all. We aim to please at Michael Hammer Investigations. Twenty-four-hour service."

"Wait a minute, Hammer, wait just one damn—"

"No." I put steel in it. "You make this happen, Alberto. I want the meet at that bar, so we're in a public place where it's harder to take me out. But it'll be after closing, so you'll be protected from prying eyes. Bring your bodyguards. In fact, I insist on that. Because I will be armed and not about to stand for a frisk or give up my piece. Get that?"

Nothing.

"*Get* that?"

The gruff voice was very soft, but I heard it all right: "We'll be there."

I hung up, let out a sigh on loan from Atlas himself, and went into the bathroom to throw water on my face. When I looked up, my reflection in the mirror looked like some crazy street bum—ragged beard stubble, bloodshot eyes, hair like dead grass. I shed my clothes where I stood, showered hot then cold, shaved, dropped some Murine in my eyes, and put on my remaining clean suit.

And the same old gun in its shoulder harness.

Now I looked like a million bucks. Or anyway one hundred grand. Just about right for a meeting I'd called of some of the top Mafia bosses in America.

I walked over. It was only a few blocks to the Betsy, and the Beach nightlife was thinned way out, with the two a.m. last call coming up soon. Couples were stumbling toward their hotels or into cabs, smiling, laughing, cuddling, the guys hoping the gals'd had enough to drink and the gals hoping the guys hadn't had *too* much. The white and pink and green hotels with their neon accents formed a surreal canyon for me to stroll through, while keeping an eye out for an ambush. That ocean air smelled just fine, and the coolness with a touch of balmy breeze whispering through the palms made South Miami Beach seem like a very pleasant place to visit.

I'd have to do that some time.

The lobby of the Betsy couldn't have looked emptier if tumbleweed were blowing through. There was a guy in a blazer at the check-in desk and that was all. Again

I was reminded of some foreign outpost thanks to the old-time furnishings, slowly whirring ceiling fans, and droopy potted palms.

The glass-and-wooden doors to the bar were shut and decorated with a hanging CLOSED sign. When I tried the doors, they were locked. I didn't have to knock before a beetle-browed bodyguard peered out at me and opened up. I went into the dim, dark wood-paneled chamber, a shallow but wide space that had its own slowly churning ceiling fan.

Behind his counter, the veteran white-jacketed, black-tied bartender looked understandably anxious. He was doing his clean-up, washing glasses, hovering at mid-bar, trying to keep as much distance as possible between him and the two factions of after-hours customers at either end of his domain.

At right seated at three tables were two bodyguards each. They were big guys in suits that had been hurriedly applied to their considerable frames, and they all needed shaves as much as I had before my impromptu spruce-up. The comical thing was that everybody was playing cards, but each little table had its own separate two-player game going. They all had bottles of Coke or 7-Up in front of them and glasses with ice. All were smoking cigarettes.

At left, in the big tufted brown-leather corner booth, the four gangland bosses sat. Hail, hail, the gang was all here. They had drinks before them but no cigarettes going and no cigars either. The entire group sat there glowering like disappointed relatives at the reading of a will. On one end was De Luca, wiry and fox-faced; then Civella with his white Caesar haircut next to Bonetti with the bushy black eyebrows and dockworker hands; and on the far end sat Meyers with his gray hair and smart-monkey features. With the exception of Bonetti, they were in the same casual shuffleboard-type attire as before.

But what Bonetti wore kind of tickled me—since he was staying in this hotel, he had just thrown on a blue silk dressing robe with a fancy AB monogram. I couldn't see under the booth's table to tell, but my money was on slippers in his case, and of course sandals and socks for Meyers.

I hadn't headed over there yet when the bartender said nervously, "Get you something, sir?"

"Yeah. A beer."

I smiled over at my invited guests, nodding to them, getting nothing back. The bartender gave me a pilsner of beer and I drank it down in three gulps.

I shoved the empty glass away, tossed a five-spot his way and said, "Blow."

He nodded, scurried out from behind the bar and went out.

I went over to the booth and pulled up a chair and sat. "My apologies for interrupting everybody's beauty sleep, including my own. But we're nearing the end of our business arrangement, gentlemen, and this one last meeting is called for."

"It damn well better be," De Luca snapped. The petulance of that would have been comical if this weren't a guy who could have you killed with a phone call.

Or maybe in my case, try *to have you killed....*

A scowling Bonetti said, "There better be a goddamn good reason, Hammer, why this couldn't wait till morning."

I remembered when I used to be Mr. Hammer.

"I wanted to make sure I was still alive," I said. "Tough calling a meeting when you're dead."

Civella said, "Might be a good thing for you to keep in mind."

But a frowning Meyers cocked his head and said, "Why do you say that, Hammer? Is Nolly Quinn trying to have you killed?"

I shrugged. "I think so. He's probably part of what happened to me tonight. Which was two heavies chloroforming me and taking me for a boat ride to be followed by a midnight swim. The intention was to feed me to the sharks. Turns out sharks aren't particular *who* gets fed to them."

Even this hardened group reacted to that kind of thing. Eyes widened, looks were exchanged, with a mutual mixture of surprise and suspicion that was just what I was after.

"Gentlemen, it's fair to say that you are an unusual consortium. You are not in business together. You are in the same *line* of business, and sometimes you cooperate, but also you are competitors of sorts. Only here in Miami it's different. Miami is neutral territory. You've come together here out of mutual self-interest, both as part-time local residents and businessmen with shared concerns."

De Luca spat, "We know who and what we are."

And so did I.

I said, "I know you do, Mr. De Luca. I only mean to point out that you are an association of businessmen, not men in business together. Accurately put?"

Bonetti said, "Get at what you're getting at."

"As affiliated businessmen, and home owners… part-time citizens here in Greater Miami… you have agreed among yourselves to obey certain rules. One of them, the crucial one I'd say, is that you are limiting your business activities in the area to largely legitimate ones. Still with me, fellas?"

Eyes narrowing under the slashes of black, Bonetti said, "Hammer…"

"So, like I say, you make certain agreements among yourselves. Like tabling for now the lucrative possibilities of using Miami and Miami Beach as conduits for certain kinds of contraband."

Now everybody sat up a little straighter. Except for one person. And that person *not* reacting was a tell that, as Pat Chambers would say, was suggestive.

"Someone," I said, "is violating that agreement."

De Luca blurted, *"Nolly Quinn!* Jesus! We been *over* this! Why the goddamn hell do you think we—"

"Quiet, Santo," Bonetti said. Soft but forceful. "Let Hammer finish…"

"Maybe we should finish *Hammer*..."

"Santo," Bonetti said with a hint of warning. Then he looked at me again. "Mr. Hammer?"

I was "mister" again.

"Nolly Quinn isn't a part of your association," I said. "But I doubt he'd go up against you... unless one or more of you encouraged him to do so. My police sources back east tell me that Quinn was in New York not long ago, looking for a partner among the five Mafia families. I think he found one. I think that partner, that silent partner, is sitting right here with us."

The simian resemblance emphasized by his wrinkling frown, Meyer demanded, "Damnit, Hammer, *who?* And what proof do you have?"

I made a casual, open-handed gesture. "First let's rule some people out. Chicago. Detroit."

De Luca and Civella visibly relaxed.

I went on: "After all, New York is the port of call for this kind of product. And we already know that Quinn is in league with one of the five families... two of which are represented here at this table."

De Luca and Civella turned to Bonetti and Meyers.

Meyers said, "And three aren't here at all!"

Bonetti said, "You pointing the finger at *two* of us or one, Hammer?"

The "mister" had slipped away again.

"One," I said. "And I wasn't absolutely sure which one of you it was..."

My eyes went from Bonetti to Meyers and back

again. Neither man betrayed a thing. They were old hands at the stone-faced Mafia look.

"...until I walked in here tonight."

Bonetti raised one black caterpillar of an eyebrow. "So you *know*, then? Who it is?"

"I'll know in a few moments. The two muscle-bound goons who came calling on me tonight were here the other day, when we had our previous business meeting. Here in the bar, I mean, where you fellas had banished your boys as a show of good faith when you called me in to hire me. Each of you brought along two bodyguards. Pretty standard. But there are only *six* with us tonight. Two are missing. The two who are being digested in the bellies of sharks right now. So tell me, Mr. Bonetti. Whose bodyguards are missing?"

The eyes of Santo De Luca, Carlo Civella and Alberto Bonetti swung like a hangman's rope toward Mandy Meyers. He sat there impassively.

"So my boys aren't with me tonight," Meyers said with a dismissive shrug. "So what?"

To the rest I said, "One creep had one of those flattop haircuts and a baby face. The other had darker hair and a pushed-in schnoz."

Those eyes were still on Meyers.

I said, "I don't feel like any great detective here, Mandy. I mean, you're the obvious choice. You're the guy who took Quinn under his wing, and brought him into the fold. You hid in plain sight by going along with the plan to hire me to take Nolly down. But in the meantime you tried to have me killed—twice. First at the Sea Breeze Motel, where two very nice civilians got needlessly slaughtered, and tonight with my one-way ocean voyage. And tell me, Mandy—were Nolly's boys after that stripper at the Five O'Clock tonight, or was it me who was meant for those slugs? Or maybe was it a two-for-one sale that didn't quite make it?"

Meyers said nothing. He seemed calm enough, but the faintest tremor was starting.

I said to the others, though my eyes remained on the little financial wizard, "I am giving you gentlemen twenty-four hours to take care of this problem, in-house. If you don't, I'm going to find Meyers here and kill everything and everybody he loves, starting with that goddamn Pomeranian, and then kill him, too, to put him out of his misery."

Looking unsettled but with his dark eyes still cold, Meyers said, "Big talk."

I grinned at him. "You're right, Mandy. You caught me. I was just bluffing." I shut off the grin. "I don't kill canines. I stick to the human species."

He was full-out trembling now, working hard at keeping his chin up. Coming apart at the seams. How many people had this little man casually sent to their deaths? Feeling nothing more than he would ordering a meal?

To the rest of the assembled group I said, "Before you give Mandy here his spanking, keep in mind there's a *second* silent partner. Somebody from the straight world, most likely. Maybe make Mandy spill that guy's identity, first."

Everybody just looked at me. I seemed to have made an impression on them, the kind I usually only make when my .45 is out.

Then, very calmly, Bonetti said, "That's all the time we need from you, Mr. Hammer. Thank you for the information, and your consideration."

Meyers, wrapping himself in his remaining shreds of dignity, slipped out of the booth and walked quietly if not steadily out.

I said to them, "I'll be happy to handle this. No charge."

All three of them shook their heads. It was so much in unison that I almost laughed. See evil, hear evil, speak evil. Only the most evil monkey had already exited.

"We'll take care of it," Bonetti said, "thanks."

"Okay then," I said, smiling and nodding at them. "I'll be wrapping up here over the next day or so. Let's not keep in touch."

And I got the hell out, glad to be walking in cool night air cut by a warm breeze, hoping they hadn't noticed my hands shaking. I told myself it was booze withdrawal, but it wasn't that at all.

Loosening my tie, I had my coat off and hung in the hotel room closet, the sling with the .45 draped on a chair arm. I was still holding exhaustion at bay—meeting with those top hoods required a high that was hanging on. But I could let go now. Could finally let go. The bed was eyeing me seductively when the knock came.

Several knocks, small, hard, insistent.

Frowning, I went over and got the .45 and moved to the peephole. At first I almost didn't recognize her, though I'd seen her just this afternoon, a lifetime ago.

Erin.

I groaned to myself. Normally a dish turning up on my doorstep was a welcome sight, but sexual hijinks right now was the last thing on my mind.

But even through the distortion of the peephole, the fashion-model waif appeared anxious and agitated. My .45 in hand, barrel up, I cracked the door, looking over the night latch.

"What is it, kid?"

She was shaking like a junkie in need of a fix. She was still in the lime-green sundress with the yellow scarf at her throat, but it didn't look fresh any more, though her make-up and that wealth of red hair remained near perfect. The giveaway was her eyes, wet and worried and red, her mascara in danger of running.

"Mike," she said breathlessly, "your Velda's in trouble."

I quickly unlatched and opened the door, letting her in, giving the hall a fast check. Nobody. I shut the door behind me and threw the night latch back in place.

With my free hand I clutched her arm. "Trouble *how?*"

"That hurts!"

I let go. I'd frightened her. She looked like a wounded bird, hugging herself with thin arms.

"Take it easy," I said softly, though fear and hate were pumping through me like high-octane gas in a fuel-injected engine. "Let's just… sit down, okay?"

With my free hand gently on her arm now, the .45 in my other hand pointing downward, I guided her to that modernistic couch where not long ago Alberto Bonetti had sat. I made a show of going over and putting the gun in its holster on the chair and coming back to sit next to her.

"How is Velda in trouble?"

"It's Nolly." She was shaking her head, the long-lashed almond-shaped eyes gazing past me into something terrible. "I think somebody *told* him, that your girl's some kind of… undercover agent, for the police? He's been at her for hours, trying to make her admit it, and tell him what she knows and what she's told and who she's told it to…"

"At her how?" I wanted to grab her by the shoulders and shake it out of her, but that wouldn't do any good. "At her *how*, Erin?"

I didn't need to take hold of her because terror already had. "He was… he's *torturing* her, Mike."

The world turned red. My head throbbed, the chloroform headache back in full force, and music was pounding in my brain, no tune, just drums hammering in relentless rhythms and instruments screeching in crazy non-melodies.

"Mike… Mike…"

I swallowed, shook it off. I didn't grab her, but my hands were fists, shaking at my sides, every cord in my neck standing out in bas relief.

"Listen, kid, if this is a set-up… if you're trying to lead me into a trap, I swear I will break you apart and nobody will ever be able to put the pieces together."

Her eyes widened in fright and her own tiny fists rose to her face and she started to gasp, sucking in air, dread gripping her and starting its funhouse ride into hysteria.

"Kid… baby… I'm sorry," I said. "I'm sorry, sorry, sorry."

She was shaking her head again. "I'm not lying, I swear I'm not lying, she's in *trouble*, Mike, you've got to help her, *we've* got to *help* her."

"Tell me, kid. Tell me!"

But all she could do was throw herself into my arms and I clutched her to me, only I was tight with rage, crazy with fear myself as I tried to console her, tried to keep everything I was feeling out of my voice as I said, "I need your help, Erin. Will you please help me?"

Her head was against my chest. She nodded. Swallowed twice and said, "Yes, yes… that's why I'm here…"

Then she sucked in air, grabbed her stomach, and flew from my arms to run into the bathroom, and slammed the door. I got up and went over and put on the shoulder sling and checked the clip and stuffed the gun back into its nest. I heard her wretching in there. A flush. Water running. Then for a while nothing.

My God, was she killing herself? Jesus, had I scared her into...

But then she came quickly out, and she had fixed her eyes where she'd been crying. I hadn't even noticed she'd hauled her little purse along, but now she was holding it up, saying, "I have keys to his place from when I stayed there."

"He might have changed the locks."

She shook her head. "No. I used the front door key today when I went over. He came to meet me there and was very upset. He said he was sorry for dumping me, and for hitting me, and that he wished he had never, ever let me go... that the Sterling woman was a bitch and betrayer and... and that he was going to get it out of her, get it *all* out of her, and then he was going to... going to..."

"Kill her."

She swallowed and nodded. "I pretended to think he was doing the right thing, the only thing he could, and he said he didn't want me seeing this, it wasn't for... tender eyes... and he sent me away, and... and I came here to *you*, Mike. I called first, but there was no answer, and—"

"Never mind that. Will you come with me? Now?"

She looked at me aghast, like Lot's wife taking it all in. "I would *never* go back inside there, I *won't*! I don't want to *see* it, *any* of it!"

I took her by the arms and held her, doing my best to keep it gentle. "Honey, I need the layout of that place. I've never been inside. I'm going to drive over there and you're going to talk. You're going to fill me in, and then you'll just stay out in the car while I go in there and…"

Her eyes got as big as their almond settings would allow and the words rattled out of her like somebody falling down the stairs: "And *rescue* her. Get your girl out of there and leave, just get her and get away from here. Right? *Right?* And you won't hurt him? Will you? You won't *hurt* him, Mike?"

"I won't hurt him," I said.

And we went.

CHAPTER THIRTEEN

Only the moonlight-muted tones of the red-tiled roof of the pink stucco near-mansion could be seen rising over the black wrought-iron gate. Those gates were slightly ajar, thanks to Erin leaving them that way, anticipating a return visit with me in tow.

I left her sitting in the Ford just down the street, as nervous as a mother with a missing child. On the short ride here she had given me the layout of the house, which was fairly simple: a single floor with an attic but no basement, not in this high water table. The walls were thick, she said, and anyone within could make all kinds of "awful noises" and no one would hear.

The wild card in her rundown was Quinn's two-man security staff—Harry and Joe, who by description just had to be the pair I tangled with at the Winter Harbor apartment where Velda had stayed till recently.

"When I left," she'd told me in the car on the way here, "they were… helping Nolly."

"Helping him how?"

A pink tongue flicked out nervously over thin red-rouged lips. "I only got a glimpse, through a half-open door. Mike, I don't want to say. Don't make me say. You promised you wouldn't hurt Nolly, and if I tell you, you might…"

"Spill or I *will* hurt him."

She swallowed. Looked at her lap. "Harry had some… some pliers and was threatening to do things… with them… to her. She already looked all… all beat up."

Words seeped through my teeth: "Which one is Harry?"

"He's got a neck brace on. Got hurt earlier this week somehow. Black hair, kind of… stupid-looking."

The caveman.

"That leaves Joe," I said. "What was he doing to her?"

"He had a… a lighted cigarette. She was on her back with her legs apart, tied by the ankles to the posts at the foot of the bed, her hands tied to the headboard, arms spread, too. Joe was… he was touching the cigarette to the insides of her thighs. Made a terrible sizzling sound but she didn't scream or… or anything. She just sucked in breath. That's what I saw him do. I don't know what else he did."

"Joe. Light blond hair? Pretty light blue eyes?"

"That's him."

The albino.

"You don't mind," I said, my jaw muscles working, "if I hurt Harry and Joe a little, do you?"

Her chin was firm as she looked out at light wee-hours traffic. "No, Mike. Not at all. Do what you want to those two. They're creeps."

Then she folded her arms to herself and shivered, though the night was not nearly cool enough for that.

"What was Nolly doing in that room, Erin, before he came out to talk to you?"

She shrugged. "Asking the questions, I guess... you know—supervising." She shook her head, gave me an earnest look. "Mike, I didn't really see much. Just enough to know I had to come find you and tell you, so you could stop it. If we're in time."

My head was throbbing in rhythm with the crazy music in my head that kept picking up tempo and spurring me on. No, I wouldn't hurt Nolly. Hurt didn't cover it.

"Mike... are you okay? You look... funny. Your eyes..."

"Don't look at them."

She clutched my right arm as I steered. "Mike! You *have* to get a *hold* of yourself. If you go in there like a wild man, you'll get killed and so will your girl. You just take it easy, okay? Just go in with a gun and bring her out."

I nodded. Managed to flick something like a tight smile at her.

Because she was right.

The white heat boiling my brain could make a fool out of me. I needed to go in cold and alert and ready. Getting even was secondary. Saving Velda was everything.

When we pulled over and parked down from Quinn's, I touched her face and said, "Thanks, kid. I don't know if I ever had better advice."

"Does that mean you'll take it?"

"No guarantees. Listen, the keys are in the dash. If I'm not out of there in fifteen minutes, or if you hear a lot of gunfire and I'm not out within a minute or so of that, you need to beat it out of here. Just scram and find a phone. Call the Miami Beach cops. Got that?"

She nodded. "You really won't hurt him?"

"No," I assured her.

That much I would do for her. Nolly Quinn deserved any agony I could lay on him, and eternity in Hell after that, but I would keep my promise and skip the fun stuff and just kill the bastard.

Now I was slipping inside the grounds through the slightly ajar gate with a revolver in hand, the long-barreled .38 I'd taken off the Cuban captain on the powerboat. The .45 was under my left arm as a back-up, but using a gun not traceable to me seemed prudent under these circumstances. Also, the .38 would make a crack in the night where the .45 would boom. The neighbors could only be expected to sleep through so much. That six-foot hedge on either side would keep eyes out, but not sound.

The landscaped front yard gave way to where the

brick driveway opened out into an area with a central lion-themed fountain that three cars were parked around. The black Caddie and the white Jag I knew to be Quinn's, the former still with a mud-smeared license plate. The white-topped red Hudson Hornet would be bodyguard transportation. That the help was still here was a kind of relief—it meant they hadn't finished with Velda.

Or anyway hadn't disposed of the body yet.

But knowing Velda, it would take them a good long time to make her talk. With fists and lit cigarettes and pliers for openers, though, she *would* eventually talk. Everybody talks eventually, unless they die first.

And that was the heart of it. They weren't trying to get where the loot was buried or where the atomic secrets were stashed or the names of her confederates. No, this was about making her admit she was a cop, that she'd gone undercover to get Quinn. After that they would want to know what information she'd already passed and to whom, but that was all frosting.

Once she told them she was a cop, she was dead. Not immediately. Not till the cake got frosted. But after that, she'd be as dead as it gets. A useless carcass to dump somewhere.

My gum-soles did themselves proud going silently across the brick to the looming house, its pinkness taking on a jaundiced cast due to sporadic yellow spots placed under the roof's overhang. Not many lights were on in there, and the feel was decidedly after hours. At close to three a.m. it should be.

A short flight of wide steps took me up to the glass-and-wrought-iron front door. Erin's key opened that and then I was in a landing-strip hallway of closets and shallow tables that led me to a big high-ceilinged front room. The decor was a bigger-budget version of the Winter Harbor pad, a white-walled world of cold wealth and pale marble floors with modern furnishings in yellows and golds. There was more framed abstract art, including what seemed to be a real Pollock this time, with a fireplace and several bookcases built into the walls. With just a handful of lights on in here, I felt like the late-night intruder I was.

With revolver in hand, I explored the house, quickly but carefully, since Harry or Joe or Nolly himself could pop up anywhere. I hit no switches, letting hallway lighting show me the way.

Every door seemed to open onto emptiness, with only two of any limited interest. One was a feminine bedroom with clothing of a smaller size than Velda's—had this been Erin's? The other was a TV room. Elsewhere Quinn had an elaborate entertainment center with a 24-inch television and fancy stereo set-up with a wall of LPs. But this modest space had a small portable TV, a squat refrigerator, and a card table with a game of solitaire going, scattered sports and girlie magazines, and overflowing ashtrays.

Here was where the bodyguards hung out, though only the memory of their cigarette smoke lingered.

In the master bedroom I found a round bed with

black satin sheets, sleek ebony furnishings, and framed paintings that were not at all abstract—stylish nudes of slender nymph-like women and muscular men, explicit in their unashamed, unabashed naked sexuality, startling in their sybaritic effect.

Velda may not have slept with this creature, but that didn't stop something terrible from crawling up my spine.

And yet the bedroom across the hall proved even more disturbing, though the furnishings and even wall art were nothing you wouldn't see in a mid-range hotel. But what else I saw made my stomach clench and mouth go dry and the crazy music in my brain start up again, distant, but there, pianissimo wanting desperately to build.

The covers had been pulled off a double bed in what had to be Velda's room—her things were in the closet, including those distinctive suitcases, and in and on the dresser. Only the bottom sheet remained, its cloth twisted as if itself in agony. Around where she had lain and forming a kind of irregular outline of her were spatters and splashes of blood, Pollock working in only white and red this time. At the bed posts were the lengths of rope that had held her, untied and hanging limp now.

At the rear of the house I entered an ultramodern white kitchen that seemed to gleam even in the dark, with glass doors onto the swimming pool area. Sounds came from out there. Somebody talking.

I moved to the glass and looked out onto the

flagstone expanse with the big kidney-shaped pool, which was lighted underneath and bordered by glowing blooms of hidden lighting in palms along the high hedge. From above the tall gated wooden fence between the patio and the dock could be seen the sparkling geometric skyline of Miami across the bay.

She was naked and kneeling, down at the far end of the swimming pool, the deep end, right at the edge of the diving board. Even from here and in limited illumination you could see the horrible things they had done to her. Her beautiful body, the high thrust of the full breasts, the sharpness of her rib cage, the sudden curve into the narrowness of her waist and then sweeping back out again, the flesh of her thighs, that beautiful tanned flesh freshly bruised in random ways, with a patternless array of terrible reddish welts and sharp slashes and dotted cigarette burns. Her face battered, bruised, her eyes puffy, the loveliness fighting to come through, her chin high, her expression defiant. Her arms were drawn back, meaning her hands were tied behind her.

Nolly Quinn, in a cream-color untucked sport shirt and tan chinos, a .22 auto in his waistband, was standing just behind her, and bouncing on the board just a little, with a hunk of her hair in his hands, like she was a dog he was walking, grinning down at her, the sophisticated face turned savage, showing its real self.

Off to Quinn's right and my left, smoking, observing, smiling, chuckling, stood his two bully boys, in Hawaiian-style sport shirts and baggy slacks and sandals. The caveman had a neck brace on, courtesy of yours truly. The albino at his side was grinning in delight, laughing and making wisecracks to his pal that I couldn't quite make out.

Nobody heard me slide the glass door open.

Down at the diving board, Quinn was bending over her saying, as silky smooth as ever, words echoing off the water, "It's nine feet deep, my love. Once you go in, it's over. I've seen you swim, sweetheart mine, and it's a beautiful sight. So sleek, so graceful. You're really an athlete at heart. But I don't think with your hands and ankles tied you'll be so graceful. Or sleek. Now, to avoid that embarrassment, you need to talk to me. Just talk to me, baby."

She spat two blood-flecked words and he yanked her head back by the hair. I could see the white of his eyes and his bared teeth.

"You stupid bitch. I *know* you were working for that son of a bitch Manley! Don't bother telling me. I should have known sooner! But you got ratted out, baby, somebody squealed on you."

So he did *know she was working as a cop!*

That meant her death warrant had already been served, that all of this slow misery would lead up to a quick kill. This process now was about information gathering. Well, that had slowed things down at least...

Still yanking her head back by a fistful of hair, Quinn snarled, "Who did you *tell*, you dumb tramp! What did you *tell* them?"

No one saw me slip out of the house. No one saw

me at all till I was half-way around the pool on their right. And it was Nolly who glimpsed me first, his eyes going so wide, his eyebrows climbing so high, it made a cartoon of the handsome features.

"*Hammer!*" he yelped.

Velda smiled. It was bloody but at least she had her teeth. It was a smile that said somebody was in trouble and it wasn't her any longer.

Harry and Joe whirled my way and they were clawing for the guns under their arms when I shot each of them in the head, dropping them to the patio floor, leaving behind little clouds of blood mist, without giving them time enough to wipe the surprise off their damn faces. I wished I could have made them suffer but knew I shouldn't screw around, and now my revolver was trained in Nolly's direction, up there behind Velda…

…only the bastard had dropped to his knees! He wasn't begging for his life, like he should have been, he was putting his captive between him and me. He still had her by the hair, yanking back, pulling her head at a harsher angle, exposing her throat to the night. He'd pulled the automatic from his waistband with his free hand, and was pointing it around her at me. Using his *left* hand, meaning he wouldn't be able to shoot worth crap with it, unless he had an ambidextrous surprise up his sleeve.

"*Drop the gun, Hammer!*"

I moved closer, keeping the revolver aimed right at him. If I could get close enough to make a fast move and get to the side of him, I'd have him. But for now Velda was between us. I was almost to the end of the pool, with maybe twelve feet still separating me from the two of them. Velda was a big enough girl that he could hide back there. If I could maneuver into position for a decent head shot, I would take it without a qualm, because that would cut off his motor skills. Would turn him off like a goddamn switch.

But all I could see was a slice of his face and the .22 in his fist and Velda blocking him from me, that prematurely triumphant smile gone from her lips.

"Drop it," he said, a coolness about it now, the surprise of me showing up something he'd adjusted to, "or I'll shove her in. Maybe you heard me tell her—it's nine feet, and she's bound by the hands and the ankles. She's a good swimmer, Hammer, but that would be a real challenge, don't you think?"

"I got a better idea," I said, nothing threatening in my voice. "You drop the gun and give me the girl. I don't need to shoot you."

"You don't?"

"No. Not at all. You see, Nolly, I exposed your silent partner to Bonetti and the boys tonight. Well, one of them."

His smile disappeared. Blood drained from his face.

"You're bluffing," he said.

"No."

I was edging forward. *Step by step*, just like the old burlesque sketch at the Five O'Clock Club. *Inch by inch.*

I said, "The whole Miami Mafia social club knows that you and Mandy Meyers have set up a Cuban drug racket in violation of their edict. Meyers is almost certainly dead by now. Probably floating by just beyond your fence."

"Why should I buy this garbage?"

"How about this, Nolly? You and Meyers tried to have me killed a couple of times tonight. Didn't go so well. Mandy's two bodyguards are shark shit by now, and when they suddenly disappeared, Bonetti and his pals noticed. Or anyway, they did when I pointed it out."

His voice sounded anything but cool as he sputtered, "I'll talk to them. That's no problem. You stop right there!"

"Here's the funny part—they already knew you were getting that racket going. Know how I know? A couple of days ago, with your late partner Meyers playing along, they hired me to kill you."

Silence but for some boat sounds from the bay.

Then: "*Try* it, Hammer. Try it and see what happens to your bathing beauty."

"I don't have to, Nolly. That's the beauty part. Bonetti and the boys, they'll do it for me."

"Go to hell, Hammer!"

"Later, thanks. But right now your best play is to put the gun down, hand over the girl, and let me walk out of here. You can pack a bag and see if you can beat the bullets out of town. It's a good offer, Nolly. Better than what I'd *like* to give you."

A nervous laugh punctuated his words: "I put this gun down, you'll kill me."

"No. Listen to me carefully. I care more about her life than your death. Is that something you can understand, Nolly?"

Velda was looking at me with lovely eyes peering from ugly swollen settings. She had said barely a damn word throughout any of this, letting me play it out. But there was love in that puffy, battered, beautiful face. I could see it. I could feel it. And only she could know what I was giving up not killing this scum.

Something flickered in his face. A hint of humanity. Had he loved someone once? But then it was gone, and he said, "No, no, you'll kill me. You're a lying son of a bitch, and you'll kill me. And after what I did to your broad here, you'll do it nice and slow. I *know* about you, Hammer. I *heard* about you."

Very quietly I said, "Then you should have known better than to go after my girl."

His smile was a curdled version of the charming one now. "But that was what made it so sweet—so *rich!* Mike Hammer's girl throws him over for Nolly Quinn. And you know what, Hammer? Now I'm throwing *her* over…"

And he did.

He shoved Velda off the diving board and she cried out, "*Mike!*" her eyes wide with terror as she tumbled off and dropped down, falling like a lovely stone into the deep end and sending up a geyser.

Nolly hopped off the board and was running on

the other side of the pool, shooting at me, little .22 cracks cracking the night. But I didn't bother firing back, pitching the revolver and diving in.

The water was as warm as a soothing bath but there was nothing soothing about the underwater sight of Velda knifing helplessly down, hair streaming like seaweed, the bubbles from her mouth going up.

It took only a few strokes to get to her and slip my arm around her waist and swim with her at my side, her body making a mermaid motion despite her bound wrists and ankles. She instinctively knew what I was doing, that I wouldn't go up to the side of the pool there in the deep end. Instead we swam underwater until we were in a shallower depth where she could get to her feet, ankles bound or not, and then we both came up gasping for air and the first thing we heard was a gunshot.

The water was to her shoulders and just above my waist as I yanked the .45 from under my shoulder, the water making it a slow-motion affair, but knowing it would still fire just fine.

Only I didn't shoot.

We'd expected to see Nolly waiting to pick us off from down toward this end of the pool, near the house, figuring that shot we'd heard had been him firing at us.

But what we saw was Captain Barney Pell in rumpled suit and hat with half a cigar in his face and a Police Special in his fist, having stepped out onto the patio where he faced Nolly Quinn, who seemed pinned in midair like a butterfly in a collection. Staring in shock at Pell, Quinn still had the .22 in his hand but the arm attached to it was doing nothing but hanging limp.

Then Quinn collapsed in a whimpering gut-shot pile.

"Guess that's what they call the nick of time," Pell said with a grin, the cigar moving side to side.

I helped Velda make it to the end of the pool and lifted her by the waist and sat her down where she could perch there with her legs in the water. No time to untie her just yet. Her expression was confused. Mine wasn't.

I sat next to her, as soaking wet as she was, the .45 casually in hand. "Velda, meet Captain Barney Pell of the Miami P.D. But don't say it's a pleasure. Because he's the guy who fingered you tonight."

Pell took a couple of steps closer to us, his friendly freckled mug blossoming into a big smile. "Well, that's crazy talk, Mike! What kind of bull are you—"

"No kind of bull, Barney. I should have known sooner, but you putting one in Nolly's belly makes it all come clear. *You're the guy who put this whole thing in motion.* You told Pat Chambers about Velda going to Florida with Nolly Quinn, knowing he'd tell me and I'd come down here and almost certainly kill the bastard for you."

He seemed genuinely amused, chuckling as he said, "Come on, Mike, you're not making sense."

But his gun was still in hand. Not quite aimed my way, but in his hand.

I said, "Nolly Quinn was a partner in crime who you wanted to get rid of. You didn't *need* him anymore. You could be Mandy Meyers' dope conduit all by yourself. Like the good old days when cops were corrupt in Miami and nobody cared. Your old buddy Wade Manley sure came to the wrong person to help him get Nolly Quinn, didn't he, Barney? He told you all about Velda, too, and you sat on that one till just today. Parceling out information to this one and that, like chum off the back of a boat."

The feigned amusement was gone now. He was shaking his head, seeming more frustrated than anything else. "This is crazy, Mike. What do I have to do with some New York cop? So I knew Manley from a convention or two, like your pal Pat. You need to settle down, brother. You need to get a grip."

I swung the .45 up at him. "I *have* a grip. *You* were the average-looking guy in a suit and a tie and a hat meeting with Wade Manley in Dirty Dick's down on the waterfront. You're exactly the guy who could set up a meeting with Manley down there and just walk right up and plug him."

"In New York? You're out of your damn mind, man. I work a Miami beat, you know that!"

I gave him the nasty grin. "But you were *in* New York last month, Barney. For the police convention. Telling Pat about Velda turning up in Miami. Passing out cigars at the Waldorf."

Pell had nothing to say to that.

"You've been keeping tabs on me, Barney, with my help. I even told you I was staying at the Sea Breeze, info that you passed along to Quinn and Meyers when you thought I was getting too close to making you as his silent partner. That got two innocents killed. That's on *your* tab."

A groan came from the fallen Nolly, who was trying to pull himself up, leaning on the .22 in his hand to do so, and Pell swung toward him and fired another shot into him, his chest this time. Quinn had been in no shape to use that gun, so self-defense it wasn't.

If these gunshots hadn't already woken the neighbors, the shrill scream that ripped everything apart surely would.

Erin Valen stood there framed in the glass doors onto the patio, her pretty little face a study in shock and rage. The redhead in the green sundress had seen Pell shoot Nolly that second, gratuitous time, and now she came running at the big cop, with no weapon but raised flailing fists.

Pell swung his .38 toward her but my .45 blew the night apart and lifted the top of his skull off before he could fire, a chunk of bloody bone sailing then hitting the flagstone and cracking into pieces. The crooked cop went down all at once, like a collapsing wall, hitting on his side, gun tumbling, cigar too, landing with his head near enough to the pool for some of what had been in it to leak out and plop down into the water. I hoped his new kid's mother married better next time.

Any stepfather would be a step up.

Nolly Quinn was in even worse shape now, not a chance in hell he'd make it, though right now he was still breathing—hard and raspy and ragged, the kind of sounds a wounded beast makes when it's crawled under a bush to die.

She ran over to her crumpled lover, held him close, weeping until the mascara and the rest of the cosmetics came apart in streaks of sorrow as he kept grabbing jagged breaths that only wracked him further, convulsions shaking them both, hers of grief, his of pain, the motion shifting the perfect mass of red hair, and I knew Nolly Quinn's secret at last.

I'd been half-right about Nolly. Earlier tonight at the Five O'Clock Club, farm girl Miranda Storsky, alias stripper Randi Storm, had tried to fill in the rest with her last breaths, no need any longer to guard a secret worth money when redemption was all that was left. She'd seemed to be bidding me "…bye… bye…" but I never was worth a damn at spelling.

Nolly was an AC/DC boy, only half gay, swinging both ways like his gate out front. But half would have been enough to get him completely killed by his hypocritical Mafia cronies, and Nolly needed the beauties he surrounded himself with to maintain his ladies' man bona fides. Only the lovelies who discovered his secret and perhaps tried to blackmail him over it, well, they had to die, didn't they? Like Kimberly Carter and Dotty Flynn and who knew how many others.

As the two doomed lovers sat awkwardly enfolded

on the flagstone, Velda and I emerged from the pool drenched and dripping, my arm around her waist. Then she reached her face up and kissed me on the mouth with heat that almost dried us off, begging silent forgiveness that wasn't necessary at all. I lifted her into my arms to carry her like a bride across the threshold into where I could unbind and clothe her.

The delicate little beauty who transcended the rest was lifting her so very handsome dying lover's hand with the gun still in it, pressing its tip against her heart, entwining her own slender fingers with his on the trigger.

"Take me with you, darling… kill me… kill me."

You could look past the askew red wig now and see the tortured face under the mask of make-up, catch the telltale clue in a graceful throat previously hidden by ribbon or high collar, look past the delicate frame of the waifish beauty and discern the houseboy who did everything for Nolly Quinn.

The sharp report was loud but not loud enough to wake Nolly, and his true love was gone too, before the poolside reverberations could even diminish.

What was it Nolly called his houseboy? Ron?

Maybe Erin was Aaron.

Like I said, I never could spell worth a damn.

A TIP OF THE PORKPIE

Part of my approach to completing Mickey Spillane's unfinished novels is to keep them in the period during which he began them, and to place them within the continuity of the thirteen Mike Hammer novels published during his lifetime.

That puts me in the odd position of working with a partial manuscript that was contemporary when written but has now become a period piece, making the end result something approaching an historical novel.

In *Kill Me, Darling*, Mike Hammer goes to the Miami and Miami Beach of 1954. To help me recreate that setting in that era, I turned to a number of books, primarily *Gangsters of Miami* (2010) by Ron Chepesiuk and *Miami Babylon* (2009) by Gerald Posner. My thanks to the authors.

I also consulted various vintage pamphlets, maps

and fliers, notably *Complete Guide to Florida* (1956) by Andrew Hepburn and *Highlights of Greater Miami* (1950 and 1957 editions) by J. Calvin Mills. Also helpful were vintage issues of *Cabaret* magazine.

ABOUT THE AUTHORS

MICKEY SPILLANE and **MAX ALLAN COLLINS** collaborated on numerous projects, including twelve anthologies, three films, and the *Mike Danger* comic book series.

SPILLANE was the bestselling American mystery writer of the twentieth century. He introduced Mike Hammer in *I, the Jury* (1947), which sold in the millions, as did the six tough mysteries that soon followed. The controversial P.I. has been the subject of a radio show, comic strip, and several television series (starring Darren McGavin in the 1950s and Stacy Keach in the 1980s and '90s). Numerous gritty movies have been made from Spillane novels, notably director Robert Aldrich's seminal film noir, *Kiss Me Deadly* (1955), and *The Girl Hunters* (1963), in which the writer played his famous hero.

COLLINS has earned an unprecedented twenty-one Private Eye Writers of America "Shamus" nominations, winning for *True Detective* (1983) and *Stolen Away* (1993) in his Nathan Heller series, which includes the recent *Ask Not*. His graphic novel *Road to Perdition* is the basis of the Academy Award-winning film. As a filmmaker in the Midwest, he has had half a dozen feature screenplays produced, including *The Last Lullaby* (2008), based on his innovative Quarry series. His documentary *Mike Hammer's Mickey Spillane* (1999) appears on the Criterion Collection edition of the film *Kiss Me Deadly*. As "Barbara Allan," he and his wife Barbara write the "Trash 'n' Treasures" mystery series (recently *Antiques Swap*).

Both Spillane (who died in 2006) and Collins received the Private Eye Writers life achievement award, The Eye.

LADY, GO DIE!
MICKEY SPILLANE & MAX ALLAN COLLINS

THE SEQUEL TO *I, THE JURY*

Hammer and Velda go on vacation to a small beach town on Long Island after wrapping up the Williams case (*I, the Jury*). Walking romantically along the boardwalk, they witness a brutal beating at the hands of some vicious local cops—Hammer wades in to defend the victim.

When a woman turns up naked—and dead—astride the statue of a horse in the small-town city park, how she wound up this unlikely Lady Godiva is just one of the mysteries Hammer feels compelled to solve…

"Collins knows the pistol-packing PI inside and out, and Hammer's vigilante rage (and gruff way with the ladies) reads authentically." *Booklist*

"A fun read that rings true to the way the character was originally written by Spillane." *Crimespree Magazine*